THE DANCING SAVIOR

THE DANCING SAVIOR

A Novel

David Hunter

CUMBERLAND HOUSE
NASHVILLE, TENNESSEE

Published by Cumberland House Publishing, Inc.
431 Harding Industrial Drive, Nashville, TN 37211.

Scripture quotations are from the King James Version of the Holy Bible.

Cover design: Gore Studio, Inc.

Library of Congress Cataloging-in-Publication Data

Hunter, David, 1947–
        The dancing savior : a novel / David Hunter.
            p.   cm.
        ISBN 1-58182-010-0 (alk. paper)
        1. Title.
PS3558.U46964D36   1999
813'.54—dc21

                                                        99-21697
                                                        CIP

Printed in the United States of America
1 2 3 4 5 6 7 8 — 03 02 01 00 99 98

To Marshall Lockhart, actress, writer and thinker.
She always defies the odds.

"We don't have theology. We dance."

SHINTO PRIEST

"Let them praise his name in the dance: let them sing praises unto him with the timbrel and harp."

PSALM 149:3

ONE

David Sage met his savior early one Monday morning in the day room of a psychiatric ward, 6 North, Municipal Hospital, Horton, Tennessee.

A short, stocky man, broad through the shoulders, and approaching middle age, Sage had a peasant body that was in stark contrast to his face. His even features had a thoughtful, intelligent look, maybe even aristocratic, at least before his nose had been broken. He was dressed in blue jeans and a checkered shirt, his standard costume even when he wore an out-of-date knit tie and a sports jacket to work.

The savior, in this particular incarnation, was one Gaynel Potts, a dwarf-like woman with frizzy hair and humped shoulders. Her disproportionately large head was accentuated by a pair of black framed glasses with lenses as thick as the bottoms of soft drink bottles. She was about forty-five years old.

Sage would never hear Gaynel claim to be the *only* child of God, though at times she did infer that she was the favorite of the moment.

She twirled in slowly that first morning as Sage sat, hands trembling, drinking black coffee from a Styrofoam cup. He tried to ignore the woman as she danced in his direction, like one of those plastic ballerinas glued to a magnetic base that skims drunkenly across the mirror of a cheap music box.

Stopping in the middle of a dainty turn, she lifted the cup of coffee from his hands and took a sip, closing her eyes and momentarily holding her breath as though she was savoring that cup of coffee beyond all other cups she had ever tasted. Her hair stood out in a frizzy halo, a home permanent gone bad.

"Good morning, my child. You look troubled," she said in a deep, melodic voice. Her expression was one of bliss. Sage would learn that she was always blissful, except when her husband showed up for a visit. During those times, she would revert to being an ordinary, frumpy little housewife with a squeaky, strained voice.

"So what else is new?" he asked irritably, getting up for a fresh cup of coffee. "As far as I know, this is the place for troubled people."

"Dance is worship also," she said, "but the scribes and Pharisees never saw that. *You* must learn to accept me if you are to be saved." She took another delicate sip of coffee and again savored it dramatically.

"Great," he mumbled, turning his chair away from her as he sat back down, "a woman who thinks she's *Jesus Christ*."

"No, no, no." She patted him from behind on the shoulder. "There was only one Jesus. Each of us comes wherever and whenever we are needed. I am sent *here* to minister with my dance. You must accept me to be saved."

David Sage turned angrily to look at her, vile words on the tip of his tongue. He never spoke them, though, for he quickly became lost in her brown, watery eyes as they stared back at him through the thick lenses, her pupils seeming twice their actual size.

"Repent and be saved," she said quietly, placing her left

hand gently on top of his head. "The kingdom is at hand."

Opening his mouth, he tried to spew out the anger that had become his social coin. Instead, he began to sob, great chest-wracking sobs of agony. There within the pale, sickly green walls of the short-term psychiatric treatment center where the air was permeated with the odors of urine, cigarette smoke, and disinfectant, David Sage broke down.

"Yes, I repent. *Please* forgive me," he begged.

"What is the nature of your sin?" Gaynel asked.

"I don't know! I *really* don't know," he cried.

"Have no fear child, when your time has come, I will save you. Wait on the Lord."

"Let's see," Dr. Wohlford said, holding Sage's chart at arm's length. A man in his early fifties, he had not yet accepted that he needed reading glasses. Psychiatrists, Sage had decided, gave in to the ravages of time no more gracefully than the rest of humanity. "This is your third visit with us in three months. Still depressed, I take it?"

Wohlford was too tall for the size of his small, bushy head. He always wore a bow tie, which only drew attention to his scrawny neck. A bad case of boyhood acne had left his face deeply pitted, and his Adam's apple bounced like a rubber ball when he talked.

"Yes."

"Have you been taking your antidepressant?"

"No."

"What *have* you been taking? The admitting physician says you were extremely intoxicated when you came in last night. The woman who brought you in told him you had

11

been talking about suicide." The psychiatrist fished a curved briar pipe out of the pocket of his tweed jacket and stuck it in his mouth, but did not light it.

"I don't remember."

"You don't remember what you were taking, or you don't remember what you said?"

"I took about fifty milligrams of Xanax over the course of an evening and drank a fifth of vodka. I don't know what I said to Jamey."

"It's dangerous mixing drugs. You know that, don't you? Of all people, you *should* know that, considering the nature of your work." He made a wet sucking sound with the unlit pipe.

Sage nodded assent.

"Anything new to report other than feelings of anxiety and worthlessness?"

"Well, nothing . . . except . . . it's not important." Sage jiggled the bait.

"*I'll* decide what's important," the doctor said, leaning forward to look at Sage the way a pathologist examines a specimen under a slide.

"My savior has appeared to me," Sage blurted out, as if with great reluctance.

The doctor's eyes lit up. He tried unsuccessfully to cover his glee at finding a psychotic symptom, where he had suspected only a dull, run-of-the-mill neurosis.

"When did this happen?"

"Well, I've been in search of salvation for some time, looking for my lost soul, I guess you could say. But it was only this morning when the savior appeared in the flesh to save me from my sins. Right here in the day room while I was drinking coffee."

"And what did the savior say?" Wohlford laid his pipe on the table and stared with rapt attention.

"To repent and be saved," Sage said. "It was a very clear message."

"Interesting." The psychiatrist picked up the cold pipe and began to suck on it again, his cheeks puffing in and out, fish-like. "You've never manifested hallucinations before."

"I know, but it was as if I could have reached out and touched the savior if I had wanted to. We were *that* close."

"Mr. Sage, as you know, we normally stabilize depressed patients and move them out as soon as possible, but I'd like to watch you for a few days to see if these hallucinations clear up or if you're going to need long-term help. I'll order something for your obvious anxiety, and we'll talk about a course of treatment later."

"Whatever you say, Doctor. I want to get better, no matter what it takes."

"All right, then." He made a note on the patient's chart. "I'll see you tomorrow."

Sage hid his delight behind a solemn mask. There was no way he was going to leave Gaynel—not until he found out if she truly could save him. He intended to keep inventing psychotic symptoms as long as necessary, for that morning as Gaynel had put her hand on his head, he had been overwhelmed by a vivid memory.

He saw a cherry wood framed plaque hanging on a bedroom wall in his grandmother's old house on Watauga Avenue. The gold and black lettering in Old English script stood out from the faded and peeling floral print of the turn-of-the-century wallpaper. As a child when he stayed overnight at his grandmother's, the plaque was always the first thing he saw when he awoke. He didn't remember when he was first able to read it, but one morning, when he was around seven years old, he had suddenly realized that he knew the meaning of the words:

Wait on the LORD: be of good courage,
and he shall strengthen thine heart:
wait, I say, on the LORD.

PSALM 27:14

David Sage had not been able to save himself, that was for sure. The vodka and the pills had not worked. Studying the Bible brought no relief. But the savior, in the guise of Gaynel Potts, had promised to save him when it was time. God had obviously been preparing him all of his life. What other explanation could there be for the plaque over his grandmother's bed, his infatuation with the Bible, and Gaynel's promise to save him if he would only wait?

"Have you thought about your soul?" Gaynel asked the old man on the couch beside her. He appeared to be about sixty and had fluffy white hair and startling blue eyes. His mouth was devoid of teeth. From time to time, he would yell, "Beal on deck! Beal on deck!" Otherwise, he remained silent, except for an occasional hearty chuckle.

David Sage listened attentively to the conversation that was taking place after the doctors' rounds and just before lunch. Most of the patients had taken their places at the card tables and were waiting on the meal cart. Since there were never enough card tables, many patients sat at the old Ping-Pong table on folding chairs, napkins laid out as if in a fine restaurant.

"There was still a lot of sailin' ships around in them days," he replied to Gaynel's inquiry about his soul.

"It's easy," she told him, reaching over to pat his arm. "All you have to do is put your trust in me and the heavenly Father."

"I sailed out of Boston in 1938 on the *Crimson Lady*, goin' to China. We was a hundred miles to sea before I knew she was a jinxed ship. The last cap'n had strangled his wife. Women on a merchant ship was *always* bad news."

"If you need more time, my son, I'll wait. Just remember I love you and the Father loves you."

"The *Tin Lizzie*, on the other hand, was as fine a ship as I ever sailed on." Without interrupting himself, the old man reached over and lifted the hem of Gaynel's dress, the pattern of which looked like the ticking from an old feather pillow, exactly like the ones Sage's grandmother had used on her beds. "I spent three years aboard her, sailed the world twice around."

As he lifted her dress, Gaynel slapped his hand away, then said in a kind, even tone: "You must focus on God, my son."

Gaynel fended off the old man twice more before a nurse's aide noticed what was happening and grabbed the old sailor's gnarled hand. "Mr. Beal! You stop that, right now! That type of behavior is totally unacceptable—and it's disgusting."

Gaynel looked up at the young nurse's aide intently for a moment, and said, in her beautiful melodic voice: "Let he who is without sin, cast the first stone."

Then, taking a deep breath, she primly pushed the dress down, got up and danced away as if nothing had happened.

"Beal on deck! Beal on deck!" the old man yelled with a laugh from deep in his chest.

Gaynel Potts, Sage decided, was, as the apostle Paul had claimed to be, all things to all men.

Two

Larry Ware punched in the electronic code, and the security lock that protected the Major Crimes Division snapped loose. The eight desks in the sprawling office space were empty, though the lights were on. Whoever had left last had forgotten to switch them off. Such a blatant lack of discipline would have sent Lieutenant Bullock up the wall in frustrated rage. A political transfer from General Assignments Division, Bullock knew nothing about solving homicide cases, which made up the bulk of the cases in Major Crimes, with some serious assaults and rapes thrown in to make sure the detectives stayed busy.

Ware, a big man with massive arms, picked up the coffeepot and carried it to the water fountain outside the office to rinse it out and fill it. He was the only black detective in the Major Crimes Division, and only one of four on the streets, except for a couple of old-timers who hauled prisoners, the former tokens in an all-white Tennessee sheriff's department.

Larry Ware had fulfilled his father's dream as well as his own. His father, "Big Larry" Ware, had been among the handful of blacks who worked for the Knox County Sheriff's Department during the turbulent era of sit-ins and marches in the sixties. He had retired without having risen above patrol officer status. The elder Ware had always believed, and rightfully so, that race had prevented his promotion.

Although Larry Ware, sometimes called "Little L" in deference to his father, was a highly respected detective sergeant at age thirty, he had his eye on bigger things. Dark-complected with heavy features, he was not a classically handsome black man in the Denzel Washington–Harry Belafonte tradition. He looked more like a young Yaphet Koto, the actor who played the tough African-Italian lieutenant on the television show *Homicide: Life on the Streets*. Ware was tough and smart, but not pretty. Fortunately, Ware had discovered during his relatively short life that a lot of women preferred rugged and tough to pretty.

The phone was ringing as he walked back into the office. He put down the glass coffeepot with a sigh and answered it. Any call coming in before seven was likely to be something unpleasant.

"Major Crimes, Sergeant Ware."

"Larry?" the husky female voice at the other end asked.

"Yeah, it's me, Jamey. Is David in trouble again?"

"I'm afraid so. They called me from Neptune's Lounge last night. David was drunk and belligerent. When I got there, he told me he had taken a handful of Xanax and drunk a lot of vodka. He was talking about eating his gun again. I'm afraid he's really going to put it in his mouth one of these nights and pull the trigger when nobody's around."

"Is he all right now?" Ware asked.

"I took him to Municipal Hospital," she said.

"Thanks, Jamey. I'll cover for him here and get by to see him this evening if I can."

"You love him as much as I do, Larry. I know you'll take care of him. Bye."

Ware hung the phone up and stood there for a moment. *If you love him so much*, he thought, *why don't you leave your husband and marry him?*

Ware's question, though, was not really fair to Jamey. She wasn't responsible for David Sage's problems, and she did go to his aid whenever he called for help.

Sage's problems had begun before he even met Jamey Olivia. The heavy drinking started during the Lyda Herrel trial—no, before that, even—when Internal Affairs dragged him over the coals for his handling of the case.

Even after Lyda Herrel had been convicted, Sage did not return to his old self. And he continued to deteriorate before his partner's eyes.

Ware looked up as the door clicked open and Lieutenant John Bullock waddled in, carrying a large cup of coffee and a bag from McDonalds. There would be enough food for three people, but the three-hundred-pound Bullock would eat it all by himself.

"Where's your partner this morning?" Bullock asked, digging into his pocket for keys.

"I'm fine, Lieutenant. Nice of you to ask."

"Why does everybody always give me a hard time?" He found the key and opened the door to his private office, where he would lock himself in and be alone with his food.

"Because you're such a deserving person, Lieutenant, I suppose. That's the only reason I can think of."

"I know you people don't like me, but I really don't care. You all think you're the Big League. 'I work for God,' and all that crap. Well, I may not be a homicide investigator, but I'm a hell of an administrator. Now, for the second time, where's your partner, Sergeant?"

"He's gonna be out sick a few days, I'm afraid." Ware

poured the water into the coffeemaker and spooned ground coffee into the basket.

"Jesus! Sage has missed three weeks out of the last three months. What's wrong *this* time?"

"Well, they're still running tests, Lieutenant. They think it may be kidney problems," Ware improvised. If Bullock ever found out why David Sage was missing so much work, he'd have the troubled detective sent to Nashville for a psychological hearing. Whether or not Sage would pass in his present condition was debatable.

"It's always something. Tell him he better get his act together or his evaluation is going to look like shit this year."

"It looked like shit last year—and so did mine," Ware replied, beginning to heat up a little.

"Don't take it so personally," the fat lieutenant said. "I know Sage has had a rough time, what with the Herrel case and his wife divorcing him, but damn it, I have a division to run here and I need *full-time officers.*" He closed the door and Ware heard the rattle of paper wrappings.

"Pompous pig," Ware muttered under his voice.

Nurse Grady and the patients gathered in a circle on folding chairs for group therapy. The walls were covered with art therapeutically created by current and former patients: drawings, paintings, and plaster of Paris plaques with homey sayings. Against the wall was a long table with folding legs that served as a surface for "art therapy" two hours a day. An open cupboard with jars of watercolors and brushes was attached to the wall over a sink. A hand-lettered sign read: PLEASE KEEP THE LID ON PAINT JARS!

"David, would you like to open today's session by telling those who don't know you a little about yourself?" Nurse Grady asked.

She was a bony, horsey woman, all sharp edges and angles, with huge front teeth always in evidence because her mouth never quite closed over them. Sometimes when she tried to speak, her lips would stick where they had dried to her teeth. Her hair was gray-blonde, pulled back in a bun so tight that her eyes stretched at the corners. She wore plastic framed glasses that had gone of style and come back in twice since she bought them. Nurse Grady was dressed casually in street clothes and a colorful smock covered in carousel horses. Orderlies and nurses on 6 North had the option of street clothes as opposed to white uniforms. Supposedly, it put the patients more at ease—with a little help from massive doses of medicine.

It was Sage's first group therapy session since returning for his current stay. Nurse Grady sometimes forgot, though, that a patient had been gone from 6 North. Sage's first two hospital stays had been three weeks apart. This last time, he had been gone only two weeks. All three trips to the emergency room had begun with drinking and pills and ended with threats of suicide—though he never remembered making them.

"No," he answered. There were three different therapy groups. Sage had joined "morning group" without being told, because that's where he had been before.

"Come, come, now, David. You're not going to make much progress at the rate you're going. You won't talk and you won't exercise and take walks with the rest of us." She had *definitely* forgotten that he had been absent for two weeks. He didn't tell her any differently.

"Exercise sessions are like gym class," he told her, arms crossed defensively. "I didn't like gym when I was in school, but

I *had* to do it. Now nobody can make me, so I don't do it."

David Sage was forty-one years old. His naturally wavy light brown hair was cut very short to keep it from looking like he'd just had a perm. The short hair, coupled with his square face and gray eyes, gave him a no-nonsense look that caused even drunken highway tush-hogs to consider carefully whether they wanted to scuffle with him, despite his mere five-and-a-half-foot stature.

"Part of getting better is learning cooperation, David," the angular nurse replied, with just a hint of petulance in her voice. "All right then, why don't *you* start the session, Edward."

"Well, I dropped a hit of acid a few weeks ago, freaked out on a bad trip, and the next thing I knew I was here. . . . And, I've been hearing voices ever since I dropped the acid."

Edward Flynn was an extremely tall, rangy man with knobby joints. His black hair, threaded through with silver, just brushed his shoulders. A red headband completed the look of an old hippie, somehow transported to the present—except, of course, at thirty he was too young to have been around when the flower children were cavorting naked and fornicating in the parks and streets. He had been a mere baby when the Woodstock Nation was at its peak.

"What's that? What's *acid*?" Katrina Close asked, twisting her lavender-colored handkerchief. She shredded two of them a day, but never ran out. Her hair was salt and pepper, cut in a mannish style. She had lost eighty pounds and was still losing. The doctors could find no physical reason for it. Her eyes had the hollow look of death about them.

"Acid is LSD, a drug that produces—" Edward began.

"Do we have to get into this crap again?" The obviously irritated speaker, a short, thin, delicate man with wispy brown hair, was Raymond Clark, a law student of thirty-eight, who had been a student, off and on, in one field or another, for more than twenty years. He smoked long, thin pastel cigarettes with jerky bird-like movements. "*Every* session ends with this lazy, archaic, pseudo-hippy talking about 'the good old days.' Everyone except him knows they're *over*."

"I resent that," Edward pouted. "I'm not lazy, I just . . ."

"Yeah"—Raymond waved his wrist delicately, a cigarette between his fingers—"then tell us the last real job you had. Nobody hires *freaks*."

"Gentlemen," Nurse Grady said, staring directly at Raymond, "the last two sessions have ended in a power struggle between you two. This is counterproductive, you know."

"I say let them go at it," David chimed in. "I'd also like to know when Edward had his last job." Raymond had not been there the previous time when Sage had been a patient. Edward, however, he was familiar with, because the pretend hippy had been on the floor during both of Sage's short stays.

"I worked on an assembly line in Charlotte, North Carolina, making radiator parts," Edward declared, his eyes glancing around the circle like a scolded puppy. "I'm perfectly capable of holding a job."

"Yes, but you *won't*," Raymond sneered, "because you're a lazy bastard who doesn't want to work. You'd rather hide in here and have other people keep you up!"

Tears welled up in Edward's eyes, but before he could speak, Gaynel got up and walked across the circle. She put her hand on his head.

"Peace, my son." She then turned and reached for Raymond.

"*Don't touch me, you psychotic bitch!*" He slapped at her with an awkward, flailing motion. David Sage was across the circle and had him by the wrist before anyone, including the detective, knew what he was doing. Raymond's eyes widened fearfully, and Sage released him almost immediately.

"Beal on deck! Beal on deck!" the old sailor shouted.

"As you sow, you shall reap," Gaynel said to nobody in particular as she danced away from the circle of folding chairs.

"I think we're finished for today," Nurse Grady tiredly said.

Raymond played the seven of hearts. Edward trumped it with the nine of spades. Sage took the trick with the ten of spades. Katrina, who had played the jack of hearts, began to move from one foot to another, even more agitated than usual. She never sat at a table, even during meals or card games, but bounced from one foot to the other in a sort of perpetual motion. "Cheat! Cheat!" she yelled shrilly. "One of you has hearts. I know it!"

"Don't be silly," Sage said. "We have to play *all* of our cards. You'd know if we cheated."

"Pay no attention to her," Raymond said, puffing on one of the long, thin pastel cigarettes. "It's time for her shock treatment. She always gets this way on the day before they come after her."

"Spades is a silly game, anyway!" Katrina hurled her cards in the air and stalked off. "I quit!"

"Did you say *shock* treatment?" Sage asked, lighting an unfiltered Lucky Strike. "As in running electricity through the brain?"

"That's right," Edward replied, bending to pick up the cards Katrina had thrown down. "In this sophisticated day of drugs and other therapy, Dr. Chavez Wilson, and other psychiatrists too, still treat patients with electroshock therapy, today euphemistically called electroconvulsive therapy, or ECT. Right now he's treating Katrina and Mr. Beal."

"I thought it was outlawed years ago," David Sage answered, taking a deep drag from his cigarette and eyeing Katrina who was darting about the large day room like a demented cartoon character.

"Nope." Edward shuffled the cards. "Every third day, early in the morning, they give Katrina and Mr. Beal something to knock them out and wheel them away to supercharge their brains. The old man comes back drooling and is quiet for a few hours. Katrina's docile for a little while, then she's back at it pretty soon, like a dog chasing its tail in circles. Hardly has any effect at all on her."

"Sounds barbaric," Sage mused, noticing that Gaynel had taken a seat on the couch beside their table. She was in one of her brief periods of rest—head back and eyes closed.

"Speaking of barbaric, why did you grab my wrist during group today? I wasn't trying to hurt Gaynel, I just didn't want her to touch me," Raymond complained in a hurt voice.

"I don't know, Raymond. Reflex, I guess. I'm sorry I grabbed you."

"Why are you here, David?" Raymond tapped a fresh, dainty cigarette on the plastic ashtray. "I'm a confused queer or a confused straight man—don't know which—Katrina's anorexic, Edward is a complete misfit. What about you? You seem so . . . levelheaded."

"I'm depressed—suicidal, they say."

"What do you say?" the aging law student asked, tilting his head questioningly, bird-like.

"I don't know, Raymond. My wife has divorced me. If my boss finds out I'm in a psych ward, he'll try to have me fired. My life doesn't work. I feel bad all the time and I abuse alcohol and other drugs."

Edward began dealing out cards for a three-handed rummy

game. "That sounds like an ordinary life to me," he said.

"What kind of work do you do, David?" Raymond asked.

"I'm a cop. A homicide detective."

"Why don't you pull yourself together? I *need* you at home. It's costin' me a fortune to have someone look after the kids. There's *nothin'* wrong with you, Gay. You just need to accept your responsibilities, that's all!"

It was evening visitation, the time between seven and nine when most working-class people did their visiting. Usually only preachers and social workers visited in the mornings.

David Sage watched as Gaynel cowered on the edge of the fake leather couch. Her husband was as big as she was small, a John Goodman look-alike who walked with an elephantine gait, perched in a ridiculous manner atop high-heeled cowboy boots with metal toe-caps and multicolored stitching. His habitual costume was a pair of blue jeans and a flannel shirt.

Sage was sure if he went down and looked at the big man's vehicle, it would be a jeep or a pickup truck with a rifle or shotgun in the rear window. To David Sage, George Potts was obviously the Antichrist.

"They miss you at church, too, Gay. We haven't had a decent organist since you came here." His voice momentarily became wheedling and seductive, or what he thought was seductive.

"I try, I try," Gaynel sobbed. Her deep, melodious voice had disappeared, replaced by a squeak that grated on Sage's nerves.

As soon as her husband left, self-assurance would return and she would become the savior again. *His* presence, however, reduced her to a quivering child, staring fearfully through her thick-lensed glasses.

"Well, you don't try hard enough!" he hissed at her. "I'm tired of living like a monk!"

"I'm sorry," she whimpered.

Sage was on the verge of intervening, though he knew it was strictly forbidden, when the loudspeaker blared out that visiting hours were over.

"Did I hear you tell Raymond that you're married, David?" Edward asked from across the darkness of the room they shared.

"No, Edward, I *was* married. We're divorced now. She said we never had a marriage because I've always been married to my job. She took my daughter and left me for a part-time English teacher at a junior college. He makes her 'feel like a woman.' At least, that's what she told me."

"How long have you been a cop?"

"Fifteen years."

"You're not really crazy, are you?"

"If I were, would I know it?"

"You don't *really* think you met the savior, do you? You're just telling the doctor that so you can stay. The way I tell him about hearing voices."

"No, I've really met the savior. By the way, it's not polite to listen in on privileged conversations between a man and his doctor, Edward."

Sage reached over and got a cigarette from the bedside table. The sedative he had asked for before bedtime had already kicked in.

"But you know better," Edward continued. "You don't actually *believe* you're talking to the savior. It's like, I keep telling them that I hear voices, but they're throwing me out soon, anyway. You're kidding them, aren't you?"

"Edward, have you ever considered getting a job?" Sage changed the subject.

"What difference would that make? *You* have a job and you're still here."

"Touché."

"I wasn't trying to score points. I just want to know if you're really crazy or not."

"Edward, would an insane person *know* if he were insane?"

"I wouldn't think so."

"Well, there you are, Edward. I don't know."

"You're a cop. Did you screw up and get an officer killed or something? Is that why you're here?"

"No! I didn't get a cop killed. I'm here because I overdosed on alcohol and Xanax." Sage's answer was sharper than he had intended.

"I didn't mean to upset you, David."

"Don't worry about it, Edward. Just go to sleep."

"All right." He was silent for a moment. "David . . ."

"What, Edward?"

"You shouldn't smoke in bed."

"I know, Edward."

And the morning and the evening were Sage's first day in the presence of the savior.

THREE

As David Sage and the other occupants of 6 North prepared to sleep, Lillith Bigman, three miles a way, as the crow flies, or seven miles if the crow had to walk on the hilly streets of Horton, Tennessee, toweled herself off and scrutinized her body in the full-length bathroom mirror.

She was still a striking woman, little changed, in fact, from the day she had first deliberately strutted by Lloyd Bigman in a white bathing suit at the University of Tennessee, at Horton Aquatic Center twenty-one years earlier. Her skin was the exact color of coffee with double cream, and her breasts still stood high, the result of religiously doing her isometric exercises that targeted her pecs.

A slight frown line appeared between her eyebrows as she turned to flex her buttocks. Not quite as firm as they could be, she decided. Maybe another half-hour a day, three times a week at the spa, but she could manage that.

Lillith had settled on Lloyd Bigman a week after arriving on campus at the University of Tennessee. She had been fortunate that she had also come to love the man she had chosen. That Lloyd had been a popular football player, a running back on scholarship, was only part of the reason she had picked him. It had been his drive and determination that had made her choose him as her willing victim.

It would have been possible for a woman of her beauty to have snared a man—black or white—with old money, even then. It would have made for an easier life, but she would not have gotten the type of man she wanted. Lillith had high standards. It was important to her that the man she married have strength of character. *That* Lloyd had in abundance.

They had slipped up during those first few passionate years, and the result had been a son, Clifford Bradford Bigman. It had been necessary for Lillith to delay her education until Lloyd was out of law school, but then she had gone back, finished college, and taken her own law degree. In time, she had become a successful corporate attorney.

She had graduated from law school the same year Congressman Fresham had hired Lloyd for his staff. After fourteen years, Lloyd practically ran the congressman's office. He was out almost every night, speaking to this group or that. Lloyd was an important man, and Congressman Fresham was getting old. It was possible, even likely some said, for a conservative black man with impeccable Republican credentials to be the next congressman from this district—unless some kind of scandal got in the way. And of late, the prevention of a scandal had become more and more difficult to suppress.

Lillith's life with Lloyd had seemed almost perfect for thirteen years—before the first episode with Clifford. Something had been very wrong with their big, strapping son, and nobody had noticed. Not Lillith, nor Lloyd, nor any of the teachers in the expensive private schools Clifford had attended.

It had begun with a call from the principal. The embarrassed woman had handed over a stack of black and white photographs. They were of Lillith in various stages of undressing. They had all been taken in her bedroom.

Rushing home, Lillith had found the place behind the full-length mirror where Clifford had cut through his closet to the back of the glass. A peephole, just large enough for an eye or a camera lens, had been scraped in the mirror. The lab work had been done in Clifford's own darkroom, which had been a present for his eleventh birthday.

When confronted with the evidence, Clifford had defiantly accused Lillith of *letting* him watch, of having known about the mirror. Before the day was over, Clifford Bigman had been placed under the care of one of the city's most prominent child psychologists, who talked of obsessions and all but accused Lillith of subliminally (or worse) trying to seduce her son.

After a year of therapy, Clifford had raped the family's cook, a woman in her mid-forties. The woman's silence had been purchased. Clifford had claimed, of course, that the woman had brought it on herself by flaunting her body. By the age of twenty, Clifford had three rapes behind him—that they knew of. And it was no longer just older women. No female was safe around him when he started prowling like a jungle cat. His "normal" periods had become fewer and fewer.

Four hours earlier, Lillith and Lloyd had returned from a private hospital in Ohio where they had picked up their son. He had seemed cheerful on the way home, laughing and joking. She prayed that Clifford was *really* well this time and would go on to become a productive member of society.

The doctors had finally become convinced, after years of probing, that Lillith had not been responsible for Clifford's dysfunction. In fact, they could find no reason for it at all, no organic brain damage and no history of childhood abuse or molestation. Lloyd had taken to muttering the term *bad seed* on occasion when referring to his only son.

Her long-suffering husband had gone to the office to check his correspondence, but a large, husky male nurse was in the room next door; Lloyd would have it no other way. At first, he had insisted on hiring an armed security guard, but had compromised with Lillith by bringing in the formidable-looking nurse, a big blond, one-time tackle for the University of Tennessee. She did not think either would be necessary. Her son seemed to be whole at last, stabilized on the new medication. In her mother's heart, she desperately wanted that to be true.

Lillith finished drying her hair in the bathroom and walked across the plush, white carpet into the master bedroom. As she sat down at the dressing table, a cool breeze hit her. She turned and saw Clifford standing just inside the sliding glass doors, having entered from the deck. Lillith snatched up her robe and held it in front of her.

"Clifford! What are you doing in here? How did you get in?"

"I used a key to get in, Mama. I'm in here because you been walkin' around nekkid again." He advanced toward her, the light glistening off his mahogany skin, the muscles rippling under his white T-shirt.

"Clifford, honey, lots of people walk around naked in the privacy of their bedrooms. For God's sake, go on back out the way you came, and I won't say anything to your father. Go now!"

He smiled, then stepped forward and ripped the robe away from her. She covered her breasts with her hands and bent forward. "Don't do this, Clifford. You don't want to spend the rest of your life locked up. This is *sick*!"

He grabbed her by the wrists and jerked her up. "Once you let me have my way—like you always *wanted* to, you ain't gonna tell *nobody*. You'll be sendin' the old man away ever chance you get."

"This is your last chance, Clifford," Lillith sobbed, "let go and get out, or I'll scream! I don't want you put away for good, but I'll do it."

"Yeah, you gonna scream, all right, Mama. You gonna scream wit' pleasure."

Lillith threw back her head and let out a piercing scream, pulling her legs together and fighting off her son. In a matter of seconds, the husky orderly came storming though the door. He hit Clifford in the back of the head with the spring-loaded blackjack that Lloyd Bigman had insisted on leaving with him.

"I'll call 911," Lillith said, as she put on her robe. "Get some restraints on him."

"Wake up, sleepyhead."

Sage opened his eyes and Jamey's wide Slavic face came into focus. Her eyes, black as anthracite, always spoke of secret jokes and laughter just below the surface. A mane of thick, straight black hair cascaded down her back. She was pushing forty-five, but could have passed for thirty.

"What brings you out this morning? You're here before the vampires." He stretched, raising his arms over his head.

"I was worried about you. Kevin is taking me to Boston on a short business trip and I wanted to see you before we left."

"Does Kevin know you're here?"

"Of course he does, silly." She lit two cigarettes, inhaled deeply, then handed one to Sage.

"What kind of man *is* he?" Sage asked.

33

"The kind who lets me do whatever I want, Lovah," she replied with a thick Boston accent, leaning over to kiss him lightly on the lips.

"I'd never put up with what he does."

"I know. That's why I'm still married to him and why you and I can only be occasional lovahs. You make me hot, but you'd smother me. Kevin is happy to just have me around."

"He lives on crumbs," Sage sneered with contempt. He had never met her husband but hated him passionately.

"I wore a new dress to the company party last night," she said, changing the subject.

"Oh yeah?" He took a drag from his cigarette and sat up.

"It was sheer and white. I didn't wear a bra." She looked at him through dramatically lowered eyes.

"Really?"

"Really. Aren't you going to ask how I kept my outrageously large nipples from showing through?"

"How did you keep your nipples from showing through?"

"With clear tape. Would you like to take it off for me?"

Sage inhaled sharply as Jamey pulled the elastic neck of her peasant blouse down, freeing both of her beautiful breasts. Her sexuality never failed to assault him like a kick to the groin. She had her back to the door and his roommate was not there, but he quickly looked to see if anyone was watching.

"Well, are you going to take it off for me or not?" Her nostrils were fluttering like a butterfly's wings. That's the way sex had been with them—volcanic, intense. He had always known in his heart that it was not a relationship he could sustain for long.

He reached forward with both hands and slipped his fingernails under the edge of the clear plastic tape. She shivered and the nipples became hard.

"Now, Lovah. Pull!" she said huskily.

He pulled the tape in one quick motion. Her round, firm breasts jiggled, and she shuddered as the tape came off. The nipples had taken on the texture of blackberries.

"*Ooooh.* That was almost like an orgasm. I've been thinking about you ever since I put it on last night."

"Excuse me . . ."

Jamey turned, breasts still free of the low-cut blouse. The pale young woman who drew blood on 6 North five days a week was standing at the door uncertainly. Her eyes darted like frightened mice from Sage to Jamey's breasts.

"Come in. I was just leaving." Jamey casually pulled her blouse up, smiled at the technician, then leaned and kissed Sage.

"Think about *that* while I'm gone, Lovah. I'll call as soon as I get back. Heah are some clothes I picked up at your apartment." She put a heavy paper grocery bag on the bed. "By the way, I brought you to the hospital in your car night before last. It's parked on the lot. The key's in the usual place under the right rear tire. And I called your partner to let him know where you are."

She walked out quickly, winking at the flustered technician as she went.

"Sorry to interrupt." The young woman's lightly freckled face was flushed as she set the wire basket containing the tools of her trade on the table beside his bed.

"Don't worry about it. Jamey just likes to do outrageous things."

"Is she your wife?" She looped the rubber tube around his arm and tapped for a vein. She had been drawing blood from him at various times over a three month period, but it was their first conversation.

"No. Somebody else's wife."

35

"*Oh.*" She was pretty in a redhead sort of way. The fine hair on the back of her neck stood up in little strawberry red wisps.

"We'll never be anything but lovers."

"Her decision or yours?" The needle slid into the vein with hardly a sting. She was good.

"Hers. I'd marry her in a minute."

"How long have you been divorced?"

"Six months. My career did my marriage in, I guess."

"What is your career?"

"I'm a cop."

The blood rose slowly in the tube, crimson against the pale backdrop of the sheets. She slipped the needle out and quickly slapped a Band-Aid in place.

"Why are you here on 6 North?"

"Depression."

"Did you OD?"

"Jamey thought I had. That's why she brought me in. I don't think so."

"Well"—she put the tube of blood on the tray and carefully labeled it—"have a good day."

"Thanks."

"Oh, by the way—" She paused in the doorway for a moment, as if something had suddenly occurred to her. "I'm off on weekends. If you'd like to go out on a pass . . . and you don't have anybody to take you, I'm not busy this weekend." The young woman seemed embarrassed, even as she said it. She hurriedly rushed out of sight, gone before he could respond, leaving an odor in the air that was like a mixture of honeysuckle and isopropyl alcohol.

"Nothing excites a woman like the smell of another female on a man," Sage mumbled to himself.

FOUR

At breakfast there were two new patients on 6 North. One was a girl no more than fifteen. She was catatonic. The staff had brought her in, shuffling spastically, mouth open and dribbling saliva, eyes staring straight ahead, and put her in a wheelchair. Her dark brown hair was braided into pigtails that dropped over petite breasts covered by a Mickey Mouse sweatshirt. Her eyes were a distinct violet color with black rings around the irises.

The second patient was a large, young black man with a bandage on the back of his head, who had spent his first two hours stalking the long hallway and muttering under his breath, pausing each time to look out the unbreakable glass panes in the center of the heavy steel doors that guarded 6 North.

He was angry. David Sage knew real anger when he saw it. The young man's rage was a murderous one, the kind that causes cops to unsnap their holsters when they meet up with it.

"Beal on deck! Beal on deck! Chow time!" the old sailor yelled as the food cart was pushed into the day room.

"As often as you eat this food, think of me," Gaynel said,

dancing by a moment later with a plate in her hand. "This is my body and my blood shed for you."

Sage got his tray and took a seat close to Gaynel. His breakfast consisted of runny scrambled eggs and undercooked bacon with two dry pieces of toast and pulpless orange juice. Patients always got whatever the kitchen sent, until a proper menu was filled out, and he had forgotten his the previous day.

Katrina brought her tray to his table but did not take a seat. She stood, shifting from foot to foot, nibbling tiny bites so the staff wouldn't nag her.

"David, eat this sausage for me. David!" she said from the corner of her mouth, like a gangster in an old movie.

"You need the nourishment, Katrina."

"Take it. I'll puke if I have to eat it."

"All right." Making certain that the nurses and orderlies weren't looking, Sage shifted the link sausage to his plate.

"Thanks" she whispered. The staff puzzled over why she continued to lose weight. Katrina always turned in a clean plate.

"That new one looks dangerous," Raymond the aging law student said as he took a seat at the table. He daintily folded a paper napkin in his lap as if sitting down in a fine restaurant. "I wonder why he's here."

"Nurse Grady told one of the orderlies that he destroyed all the furniture in his father's house," Katrina said.

"I didn't think they allowed violent people on 6 North." Raymond looked in the new patient's direction and shuddered, his delicate hand fluttering upward to touch his chest nervously.

The young black man was at a table alone, devouring his food and glaring at everyone. His eyes flashed as he noticed that Raymond was looking at him.

"What are you starin' at, peckerwood?" the young man growled.

"See," Raymond said from the side of his mouth. "He's dangerous. I don't think they should allow dangerous people on 6 North."

"Probably just waiting on a court order to send him to another facility," Sage reassured him.

"Well I hope it's *soon*." Raymond lifted a dainty bite of French toast to his mouth.

"Beal on deck. Beal on deck!" the white-haired old sailor yelled again, then chuckled uproariously. He was in rare form.

"*Shut the fuck up, old man!*" The new patient stalked over and stood in front of the elderly sailor with the startlingly blue eyes and stared down at him, fists balled at his sides.

"Beal on deck. Beal on deck!"

Clifford Bigman slapped the old man across the face. The cracking sound grabbed Sage's attention and he was out of his seat without thinking. As two orderlies charged across the room, Sage remembered that he was not responsible for keeping order inside the ward and sat back down. All he had to do was take his pills and wait for salvation. The old man merely stared at his assailant in stunned silence.

"Get your hands off me, man! I don't have to listen to this old bastard. I got rights, too," Clifford Bigman yelled, just before the two orderlies took him to the floor. A third orderly jumped in a moment later.

"Take him to his room and restrain him," said Nurse Grady, who had appeared almost instantly out of nowhere. "And get an injection ready."

Most of the patients went on eating as if nothing out of the ordinary was happening, while the young man, screaming curses, was dragged off to his room where he was restrained to the bed with canvas straps.

For several minutes, he continued to scream and curse.

When he finally stopped, the other patients knew they had given him the magic injection.

So began David Sage's second day on 6 North.

Detective Larry Ware lowered himself into the wooden chair at his desk. The ancient screws and joints of the old piece of furniture protested loudly, but nobody was there to comment on it.

His fellow morning-shift detectives were just stopping off for their morning fix of cholesterol and caffeine. Ware was not early; he had become involved in a shooting case just before the end of his shift the day before, which had taken him all the way through *second* shift. He had not even made it to the hospital during visiting hours to see his partner.

Then, on the way home, a serious domestic assault had taken place near his location. Recognizing the name of the complainant as being the wife of Lloyd Bigman, a heavy-weight congressional aide, he had taken the call, which had now carried him into his twenty-third hour on duty.

His tenacity, punctuality, and willingness to work extra hours, he was convinced, were the chief qualities that had made him the first black Major Crimes detective with the sheriff's department. Being a cop, Ware had discovered early on, was harder for a black man than for his white counterparts, except in one respect—white cops had to learn what it felt like to be a nigger, while black men grew up knowing.

Cops are members of a distinct subculture, Ware had quickly learned, hated by the very poor, sometimes respected by the lower middle class, but only tolerated by the upper classes. He also understood that after a while all good cops bleed blue. Race becomes a secondary issue to being a respected cop.

Larry took a deep breath, then another sip of bitter black coffee and reread the report in front of him, the one he had answered on his way home. It had been a potential hot potato that a rookie detective might have dropped.

Clifford Bigman, the young man involved in the assault, who had been taken to Municipal Hospital for stitches and a quick examination by a private psychiatrist, was one sick, dangerous puppy. He was also the only child of Lloyd Bigman, the most powerful black leader in the county, maybe in all Tennessee, who insisted that the problem be handled as a medical incident, not a criminal act.

Larry Ware had done Lloyd Bigman's bidding, not because he was easily pushed around by powerful men but because he genuinely respected the congressional aide and felt sorry for his wife, a beautiful, classy lady, who had sat and sobbed as she told Larry what had happened. The bruises on her arms told the tale as vividly as her faltering words and downcast eyes.

Such fine people didn't deserve a son like the one they had gotten. Besides, the detective knew Clifford Bigman would be locked up longer in a psychiatric ward than if he were jailed. A judge might not believe what the boy had *really* attempted. Most people don't even want to *think* about twisted individuals like Clifford Bigman, let alone hear about their evil deeds.

Larry Ware had "neglected" to put a copy of his offense on the press board, which reporters check early every morning. It was a violation of departmental policy, but a good cop knows when to bend those regulations. Someday an up-and-coming cop like Larry Ware might need a favor from a congressional aide. Maybe Lloyd Bigman would even be the first black congressman from East Tennessee, if you could believe rumors.

Ware was about to leave when he noticed an open file on his partner's desk. It had apparently been there all along, but he had not noticed it until now. It was the Lyda Herrel file. On top was a letter from the Department of Corrections notifying Sage that the principal in one of his cases had been released from the women's correctional institute pending a new trial, assuming there was a new trial.

Ware closed the file thoughtfully, speaking aloud to himself. "Lyda Herrel getting out of prison. *This* must have been what put David back in the hospital."

Sage sat waiting quietly for Dr. Wohlford as the psychiatrist made his morning rounds of the day room. He wondered if he should tell the doctor about the dream that was part of the *real* reason for his excessive drinking and pill-taking.

He had the dream often, always aware that it was a dream but unable to wake up. It was the second recurring dream of his life. The first had been about a large, hairy animal, a bear or gorilla; sometimes it was one, sometimes the other. He had lived with that dream from early childhood until he was twenty years old.

His grandparents had lived in Merlin Heights, a part of old Horton, on a hillside that dropped off sharply to the sidewalk. The children of the family were constantly warned not to go around to the front, especially not on tricycles, bicycles, or any other wheeled vehicle. It was ingrained in them as soon as they were able to walk.

This was the setting of his recurring dream where he was frequently chased by the large black animal. Playing quietly in the back yard, he would hear a noise and turn to look. The beast would be moving toward him from the alley, gaining speed as it came. David would speed away on his tricycle, pumping as hard as he could, breath hissing in and out, the creature closing in on him.

Hurtling alongside the house, past the iris bed he would go, gaining momentum. Then he would look back over his shoulder and see the creature—he could not decide if it was bear or hairy primate—again closing in on him.

When David looked forward again, he would be going over the embankment. Horror would seize him as he hit the empty air and began to plunge downward. He had always feared he would die during the dream. He had even heard one of his aunts say that he would if he ever hit the concrete sidewalk before waking. He never did hit the ground, though, not until the last time he had the dream.

At twenty, he dreamed the dream for the final time the day after his father died, ending a love-hate relationship of long standing. David's father had loved him, but he never liked his son very much. The studious boy had been a disappointment to him. He wanted a practical young tradesman, but got a dreamy-eyed poet instead. He didn't live long enough to see the man that David eventually became as a result of constant verbal and physical abuse—a man as brittle and unmoving as carbon steel, at least on the outside.

David was riding his tricycle as usual that last time he dreamed the dream, and the black horror was bearing down on him. He turned to look at the creature over his shoulder, but there was no bear or gorilla, only his father, grinning the way he did when he would hear David get up in the night to go to the bathroom. He would wait in the dark hallway to grab his son and laugh at his screams and futile struggles. It was always great fun for the elder Sage.

Turning that last time, David found himself hurtling into the air over the sharp embankment. Something was different, though. He was not afraid because he somehow knew that he was in control—and having the dream for the last time. The ground rushed up, but when he hit it he bounced like a soap bubble. Landing lightly on his feet, he looked up the hill and smiled.

The black beast suddenly transmogrified into his father, who—upon seeing that his secret was out—had recoiled, fear in *his* eyes, and run back the way he had come. In the South, it is often said that a boy can never be a man until his father dies. David Sage believed it.

Sage never had that dream again, but the new one, which had come upon him in his fortieth year, was every bit as terrible.

In the new dream, there was a tunnel—a long, dark, damp tunnel. As he walked through it, on each side of him eyes glowed ruby-red in the darkness. He did not know what kind of creatures were behind those eyes, only that he had to stay in the middle of the tunnel or be ripped apart.

When he reached the end of the tunnel, he opened a wooden door. On the other side was a young woman with an angelic face. She was always naked, standing with her right side toward him. Her skin was as smooth and fine as porcelain. Her pale, pink nipple, which stood erect like a strawberry in a dish of cream, caught his eye and held his gaze.

She reached out and took his hand, then turned slowly. The other side of her body, the part that remained hidden until she turned, was too hideous to bear—mutilated, shredded flesh and bone showing through, with tendons and muscles writhing like snakes. Sage would try to pull away, but couldn't.

Her grip was like a tempered steel band. He could smell the distinct odor of blood as she pulled him toward her. He would suddenly realize that she was about to kiss him on the mouth with her lacerated lips.

"You would have been better off with a millstone around your neck," she hissed through twisted, smiling lips, sending chills of terror up his spine. "Come and love me."

Just as the ragged and bloody mouth was about to meet his, Sage would scream and wake up sweating. After nearly a year, the dream was as unavoidable and real as it had been the first time.

Sage was certain he could not survive twenty years of the second dream, but he had decided nonetheless to keep it to himself—for a while at least. It would only complicate matters if he confided in Dr. Wohlford. Besides, his salvation would not come through the doctor. It would come through the doctor's patient, Gaynel Potts.

As Sage sat thinking of the dream and its horror, Wohlford folded his lanky body into a chair near Gaynel who was on the couch next to Sage's table.

"Gaynel," Dr. Wohlford said, "you're going to have to cooperate with me. The nurses say you carry on conversations with your husband. If you can talk to him, you can talk to me."

"What is your wish, my child?" she asked, smiling sweetly.

"I want you to talk to me about what's on your mind. We can't keep you here forever. This is a short-term ward. We'll have to send you on to the state hospital if you don't let us help you." Dr. Wohlford's Adam's apple tended to jump more rapidly as he became excited. He was wearing a blue and white polka dot bow tie.

Peering from behind the monstrously thick glasses, Gaynel answered, "I am here to heal, not to be healed."

"Have it your way, but I'm warning you, we can't go on forever like this. Your husband is not happy with your progress."

Gaynel flinched at the mention of her husband but did not speak. She only nodded at the lanky psychiatrist wisely.

Wohlford let out an exaggerated sigh, then unfolded his long, lanky body from the metal chair. He picked up his clipboard and moved over to Sage's table.

"Well, David, your nurse tells me you're not cooperating. She says you refused to go for a walk yesterday and that you won't do your exercises."

"That's right."

"Why not?" He swallowed hard and the bow tie jumped up and down.

Sage shrugged. They had discussed it before.

"Are you still in contact with the savior?"

"Yes."

"What does the savior look like?"

"I can't give a description of things spiritual," Sage lied, having no intention of telling the doctor about Gaynel. His experience had taught him that if a disease can be pinpointed, doctors will try to cure it. Sage did not want to be cured. He wanted to be *healed*.

"I'm going to put you on a new medication this afternoon, Mr. Sage. I think it will clear up this obsessive thinking."

"Thanks a lot," Sage replied.

Across the room he could see Dr. Chavez Wilson talking to the old sailor. The doctor appeared to be getting no more response than anyone else could get from him most of the time. Wilson was the opposite of Wohlford—a short block of a man with the sloped shoulders of a Neanderthal. His hair was silver and worn in the wavy "ducktail" fashion of his youth. He sounded remarkably like a used car salesman trying to close a deal as he attempted to coax a response from the old seaman.

The angry black youth had been let out of restraints after lunch. He entered the room, his amber eyes surveying the ward like a hungry panther. His eyes paused on the newest patient, who was even louder than the old sailor.

"Has anyone seen my wife?" he screamed out in a hoarse voice, eyes darting about in terror. Mr. Yow was a roly-poly little man in his fifties and Caucasian, despite the oriental-sounding name, with gray hair clipped short in a buzz cut. When his wife was there, he never acknowledged her, even when she sat and patted his hand, but as soon as she left he would cry out for her like a lost child.

"You're all a bunch of pasty-faced, peckerwood lunatics," Clifford Bigman announced to the room at large. When nobody responded, he snorted in contempt and stalked back to the small refrigerator where the dietary staff left snacks for the patients. Each was labeled with a patient's name.

"Let's see, what *do* I want," he said loud enough for everyone to hear him, staring at them slyly out of the corner of his eye.

"Doesn't matter what you *want*," Katrina snapped from the table where she was playing cards, even though she had not the slightest interest in the food that was in the refrigerator. "You only get what the staff leaves with your name on it."

"Who the hell do you think you're talkin' to, you ugly old ho'? I *take* what I want." He picked up two half-pints of chocolate milk and tore one carton open. Swallowing it in a gulp, he opened the other and walked over to the table where they had left the catatonic young girl with the long braids and violet eyes. She was still not communicating, but her mouth was no longer hanging open.

"So what's your name, Sweet Cheeks? You the only purty thing in this dump. You want some choklit milk?" There was no response from the girl, of course. The young man leaned in closer, his eyes becoming slits.

"Hey! I'm talkin' to you, bitch!"

"Mr. Bigman, Rachel can't hear anything you say." Nurse Grady stood over him, hands on hips.

"Get the fuck away from me, you old slut. Don't ever git in my face!" He stood up, towering over her. Two orderlies quickly moved in their direction, but the big-boned nurse stood her ground.

"You will not intimidate anyone in *this* ward, Mr. Bigman. If you try it again, you'll go back in restraints."

They stood there, the rangy, horse-like Nurse Grady and the fierce young black man. He was the first to blink.

"I ain't tryin' to *in-ti-mi-date* nobody." He raised his hands placatingly. "I wuz just tryin' to be friendly wit the young lady."

"He tried to rape his mother, you know," Raymond said primly. "That's why he's *really* here."

"Who tried to rape his mother?" Edward asked.

"The black guy," Raymond answered. "I heard the night nurse and the clerk talking about it this morning. The excuse they used to get him admitted was that he was breaking up the furniture, but it's not true. He has a long history of sexual problems."

"Look who's talking about *sexual* problems." Edward laughed, shaking his shoulder-length hair across the back of the chair.

"I may be a *queer*, but I never hurt anybody!" Raymond shot back. "And at least I haven't burned my brain with chemicals like some people."

"Did you say he tried to *burn* his mother?" Katrina asked,

bouncing from foot to foot. Her cadaverous face was becoming thinner every day. Dr. Chavez Wilson was threatening her with forced feeding.

"No, Katrina. I said he tried to *fuck* his mother."

"What a horrible thing to say, Raymond," Katrina snapped. "I don't believe it for a minute. A person would have to be *crazy* to want sex with his mother."

FIVE

They were once more gathered, folding chairs in a circle, for group therapy in the same room that later would be used for art therapy and music therapy. It was the same group as from the previous day: Raymond, Edward, Katrina, Gaynel, the old sailor Mr. Beal, Nurse Grady, and Sage. In addition, there were two more faces: the young black man and the gentleman who kept calling for his wife. He was at the moment having a period of lucidity. A husky orderly was also present, presumably in case the young man got out of hand again.

"Good morning, group," Nurse Grady said. She was wearing her smock with the carousel horses.

"Good morning," Katrina and Raymond answered dutifully.

"We have two new members this morning," Nurse Grady continued. Her upper lip slid roughly over her enormous front teeth. "I'd like to have them introduce themselves and tell us a little about their lives. Would you go first, sir?" She nodded toward Mr. Yow.

"My name is Lawrence Yow," the little man said, "I operate a construction business. I've been feeling a little depressed the last few weeks, so that's why I'm here." He nodded to show he was finished. There was no sign of the frantic little man who had been running around screaming hoarsely for his wife earlier in the day.

"And you, please." She indicated the black youth.

"If I play this game, does it mean I'll get out of here?" The young man sat with his arms crossed, a sneer on his face.

"That's up to your doctor, but I *can* tell you that you'll never get *better* unless you help us help you," Nurse Grady answered, using one of her favorite lines. As far as Sage was concerned, group therapy was a lot of crap. Unfortunately, it was also unavoidable.

"I'm already as good as I can get, but I guess they'll keep me locked up forever unless I play your silly little game. My name is Bigman—Clifford Bigman. I'm twenty, and I'm locked up in here because my father's jealous of me. He's old and weak, and he can't stand to look at me because I'm young and strong."

"That's a good start, Clifford."

Nurse Grady looked over at Sage as if to say, *You can't stall any longer, Mr. Sage.*

"My name is David Sage, forty years old. I'm a cop, a homicide investigator. I'm here because I overdosed on drugs and alcohol." He glanced across the circle and saw that Gaynel was sitting with her head back and eyes closed, the way she usually sat when she was not dancing.

"*Very* good, David. Now, this morning we're going to play a game called, 'I wish.' Who'd like to start? Edward has his hand up, so he'll begin."

"I wish these voices I keep hearing would go away. I can't focus on anything these days and they keep me awake at night." He looked around for sympathy, but was met, instead, with a bunch of blank stares. He had been informed that he was being discharged at the end of the week. He glanced at

Raymond, waiting for a sharp reply, but none came.

"All right. Raymond?" Nurse Grady said with a nod.

"I wish I could be like David."

Sage looked at him, startled. The aging law student was, as usual, neatly dressed in khakis and a pink pastel shirt. His fine brown hair was impeccably combed, as if ready for a job interview.

"And why would you want to be like David?" the nurse inquired eagerly, sensing a revelation.

"Because he's a *man,* and nobody ever doubts it. Even here, he keeps his cool and isn't afraid."

The young black man snorted from across the circle.

"Do you have something to say, Clifford?" Nurse Grady asked.

"Yeah, Nurse. I got somethin' to say about that. Cops just *look* cool. Unless they got a piece, they ain't *shit.*" He looked at Sage, a challenge in his pale amber eyes. "I see a short man with a buzz cut and no neck. Looks like a *fireplug* to me."

"Do you have a reply for Clifford?" the nurse asked Sage, eyebrows raised.

"No. I'm used to people like Clifford. Listening to them is like listening to the wind blow."

Clifford stiffened in his seat. His eyes flashed and nostrils flared, but he said nothing. "But I *would* like to remind Raymond that I'm here for the same reason he is—because I can't cope outside."

"I think that was a good, honest exchange. Now, Katrina."

"I wish I could get out and go back to work." The bones were actually beginning to show through the tightly stretched skin across her cheeks. She twisted rhythmically in the seat, ripping up a fresh lavender handkerchief, because Nurse Grady would not allow her to stand during group.

"Katrina, you can leave the hospital whenever you wish," Nurse Grady said quietly.

"I know." She became silent, but the twisting intensified. The first lavender handkerchief of the day disintegrated in her hands. "But I'm not ready yet," she said, looking down at the floor.

"Gaynel . . . Gaynel! You have to participate. Open your eyes! Do it *now!*" the nurse snapped impatiently.

Gaynel's eyes popped open, magnified by the thick lenses of her glasses. "Yes, my child?"

"We're playing 'I wish.' What do you wish?"

"I wish for nothing." Gaynel smiled sweetly, almost bringing tears to Sage's eyes. "I am here to do my Father's will, not to make silly wishes."

"What is your Father's will?"

"You already know that, my child. I dance for the salvation of others."

"No, Gaynel, you dance to shut out the world. You won't face what's wrong. And until you do there's no hope for recovery."

"The scribes and Pharisees didn't believe me when I was Jesus either. Few recognize the Christ Spirit when they see it. But those who *do* find salvation. God has taken the weak things of this world to confound the mighty."

Gaynel looked directly at Sage as she spoke. *How self-assured she was! How different from the cringing housewife she became in her husband's presence.*

"Very well," Nurse Grady sighed. "What do you wish, Clifford?"

"I wish women wouldn't paint theirselves like whores. It makes me *want 'em.*"

Everyone turned toward him, shocked that he had answered in a civil tone. He was staring ahead, as if lost in thought. The light of the overhead bulb gave a glistening cast to his dark skin.

"Can you explain that, Clifford?"

"What's to explain, Nurse? They *know* what it does to us, but they still paint it on. And they let us look at their bodies, then say *no*."

"Who does, Clifford? You must have somebody particular in mind." The nurse leaned forward.

He started to answer, then his pale amber eyes narrowed. "You want me to say somethin' crazy, don't you? Maybe somethin' 'bout fuckin' my mother. That's what you want. Right?"

"No, Clifford. I just want you to say what's on your mind."

"I've said all I'm gonna say. You just tell that Dr. Wohlford that I cooperated with you."

"I'll do that, Clifford. Mr. Yow, what do you wish?"

Mr. Yow was smiling. He looked almost cherubic with his close-cropped gray hair. They all turned their eyes to him.

"Well . . . I wish my wife would come." His face suddenly twisted. "*Has anybody seen my wife?*" he screamed out in his strained voice. "*Has anybody seen my wife?*"

The orderly escorted Mr. Yow away, still screaming hoarsely.

Gaynel stood and did a graceful pirouette toward the door. Katrina stood and began to shift from foot to foot. Nurse Grady acted as if she intended to say something, but instead she dismissed them all with a wave of the hand.

Group therapy was over for the day. Mr. Beal didn't get the chance to make his wish, but nobody seemed to notice.

Mr. Yow walked over and stood in front of the chrome and plastic chair where the woman with the blue hair was sitting. She visited Katrina almost every evening. There was a general consensus among the patients and staff that she was the femme half of a long-term relationship. In contrast to Katrina's short hair and masculine dress, the woman was the picture of femininity. It was only speculation, though. Katrina never discussed her sexual orientation.

The woman looked up and smiled at Mr. Yow. It was the kind of smile normally reserved for children. "How are you?" she asked. The woman was in her late forties or early fifties.

Mr. Yow did not reply. He was in one of his quiet phases. The woman's eyes opened wide and she gasped as Mr. Yow unzipped his pants, displayed a formidable penis for such a small man, and proceeded to urinate in her lap. Her mouth formed a small "O," but she said nothing.

"Mr. Yow!" one of the night orderlies yelled. "*Stop that!*"

Startled, the little man looked around, as if waking up from a sound sleep. He looked down and, seeing what was happening, bent and turned as if trying to cover himself up. Twisting this way and that, he looked for a place to hide. The stream of urine scattered patients and visitors as it arched in a circle around Mr. Yow.

"I say this for the little man," Clifford Bigman said, laughing for the first time since they had brought him in, "when he say 'piss on you,' he *means* it!"

"Dave?" The voice came from across the darkened room, seemingly disembodied.

"What, Edward?" Sage asked, taking a deep drag from his cigarette.

"That was pretty funny what Mr. Yow did tonight."

"Yeah, it was. I think Katrina's friend will be a little nervous about visiting from now on."

"You really shouldn't smoke in bed, you know."

"I know, Edward. I really shouldn't."

"They're kicking me out, David, and I'm not cured. The voices are still there."

"Nobody believes that you hear voices, Edward."

"You don't believe it?"

"No."

"Well, I *do*."

"Whatever you say, Edward."

"I'm thinking about killing myself," he said.

"And how will you manage that?"

"I could jump out the window. It's six floors down."

"There's a double layer of safety glass, Edward. I don't think you can get through it."

"A sick and desperate man can do anything, David."

"Whatever you say, Edward. Let's get some sleep." Sage put out his cigarette and rolled over on his side.

SIX

The ward was always quiet at six o'clock in the morning. David Sage shuffled in house shoes to the day room for his first cup of coffee, nodding at the night nurse and orderly who would not go off for another hour. He had never had a conversation with any of the night-shift people. Working nights in a psychiatric ward is like being a prison guard. The staff only gets to know the troublesome inmates.

He was surprised to see both Edward and Raymond already at the table next to the coffee urn. Despite Raymond's avowed hostility to the old, pseudo hippy, they were nearly always together.

"Good morning," Raymond greeted them.

Sage nodded and drew a cup of bubbling black brew from the large urn. The urn would be filled many times during the day. As he sat down, an orderly rolled the old sailor in and parked him by the door. He was slumped forward, saliva running from his mouth, still unconscious.

"Mr. Beal is back from his shock treatment," Edward said. "They'll be wheeling Katrina in shortly. When Katrina gets back, Dr. Wilson will come in and look at them. I don't know why. They're *always* unconscious."

"Why does the doctor do that to them?" Sage asked no one in particular.

"It doesn't do any good to ask," Raymond replied. "The doctors don't even know. In the beginning, back in the thirties, it was believed that epileptics never became schizophrenic. The theory was that if convulsions were induced, the schizophrenia would go away."

"Is that true?" Sage inquired.

"No," Raymond replied, waving his thin, delicate cigarette as he spoke. "In fact, electroconvulsive therapy—they call it ECT—is now used mostly for depression, not schizophrenia. Personally, I think Dr. Wilson gets off on watching people suffer."

"Yeah," Edward interjected, "it looks pretty bad. I saw a lot of it when I was in the hospital down in Georgia. They put electrodes on the temples and zap the patient with 110 volts for about a half a second. They sometimes convulse and jerk something awful, even after they've had anti-convulsants and anesthetic."

"A 110-volt current?" Sage said with a shudder. "Why doesn't it kill the patient?"

"Well, there's 110 volts but the resistance is only a couple hundred milliamperes," Edward told them. "Resistance is what kills. There's very little resistance, and it's of short duration."

"Leave it to Edward to know as much about shock therapy as the technician," Raymond said sarcastically.

"I pay attention, that's all." Edward sounded hurt. He shook his black and silver mane of hair angrily.

"Does this shock treatment ever work?" Sage asked.

"Oh, yeah." Raymond took a sip of coffee. "Sometimes it's dramatic. One of the old theories was that it satisfied a patient's desire to suffer. I even heard a Pentecostal preacher say once that the electricity worked by driving out demonic spirits. Nobody knows for sure *why* it works. But it *does* work sometimes."

"It doesn't seem to be doing much for Katrina or Mr. Beal," Sage observed, moving over to refill his cup.

"Sometimes it takes a few weeks," Edward said.

At that moment, Gaynel whirled in, arms lifted like a ballerina. Sage smiled to himself as he watched her. Just behind her, Nurse Grady and one of the day orderlies led in Rachel, the catatonic fifteen-year-old. She shuffled, eyes still wide in hidden terror, and allowed them to sit her down. Someone had overheard a nurse say that the child's mother had been killed in a car wreck.

She would chew and swallow what was put in her mouth, and use the toilet when placed there, but otherwise she didn't communicate with anyone. She was a strikingly beautiful child with her violet-colored eyes. Every evening her father, a youthful-looking man in his mid-forties, would sit and hold her hand, talking to her with tears running down his face.

"Well, it sounds like breakfast is here," Raymond said as the food cart clanged its way down the hall toward them.

SEVEN

Katrina stopped at the table where Sage was sitting with Raymond. Tilting from one foot to the other, she leaned over and propped her elbows on the table. She had been quiet through breakfast and morning therapy, but as lunch approached, she was back to normal. The shock therapy was wearing off faster after every treatment. She whispered in a conspiratorial tone, "Clifford has escaped."

"How do you know?" Raymond asked.

"I heard the ward clerk calling Security. Nurse Grady is frantic."

"How did he get out?" Sage asked.

"He kept walking up and down the hall. When the ward clerk opened the door to get the mail, he just pushed his way out and ran to the stairway."

"Good riddance, I say." Raymond sniffed.

"I heard something else, too." Katrina looked at them smugly, waiting for a response.

"What, for God's sake? What else did you hear?" Raymond snapped.

"The clerk told security that Clifford should never have been sent to a minimum security ward because he's too dangerous."

"We knew *that*," Raymond told her.

"There's more. Clifford's father is a lawyer on Congressman Fresham's staff. It seems the congressman has been keeping Clifford out of jail for years. He did his first rape when he was sixteen."

"There's something going on down in the parking lot," Edward yelled from his seat by the window.

They moved over to look outside, including Gaynel, who whirled over gracefully, and Mr. Yow who seemed to be having a coherent moment. The windows of 6 North looked directly out onto the parking lot of Municipal Hospital. Four men in uniform had surrounded a lone black man, like wolves taking down a moose. He was whirling and fighting desperately.

"That looks like Clifford," Edward said with a laugh.

"It *is* Clifford," Raymond told him. "He escaped."

"Why would he do that?" Edward sounded genuinely puzzled.

"Because not everyone wants to spend their lives locked up like you do, Edward."

"I don't want to be locked up forever," Edward snapped indignantly. "Just until I'm *well*."

"They've got him!" Katrina yelled. "Wait . . . No. No, he's loose again."

Sage watched the scene unfold with professional interest. It was obvious that the security officers were not real street cops. One of them could have quickly disabled Clifford with extreme pain but little damage if they had known what they were doing.

"They've got him pinned. They're cuffing him!" Edward relayed, even though they could all see for themselves what was happening.

"Well, I guess that's that," Raymond declared.

"Not if he keeps resisting. It could take a half-hour for them to even get him to the building—the way they're doing it anyway," Sage observed.

"How would *you* do it?" asked Raymond.

"I'd get on a pressure point and make him glad to be moving."

"I'll just bet you would, too." Raymond was looking at David Sage with undisguised hero-worship.

"It's no big deal, Raymond. I'm trained to handle violent people; you're trained to practice law. It's all in the training."

"It doesn't take a lot of courage to practice law. I'd *never* have the courage to fight somebody like Clifford. That's how I became a queer, you know." Suddenly Raymond was sobbing. "I thought if I did what they wanted, they'd leave me alone."

Before Sage could respond, Raymond ran out of the room.

"Medicine time," Nurse Grady said from the door. "The excitement's over. They're giving Clifford a shot down in the emergency room. Line up for your medication."

He was a truck driver, Sage had heard him tell one of the orderlies. But he looked like an aging bartender from a "B" grade Western. His blue-black hair was obviously dyed, and his little mustache was neatly trimmed, a sooty line about a quarter of an inch high and ending short of the corners of his mouth. They had brought him in from the emergency room right after breakfast, and he had slept through lunch.

"I don't belong here," he told the orderly. "I just had too much to drink last night."

"Your wife told the doctors you were suicidal," the orderly replied.

"That's crap," he said.

"It may be," the orderly acceded with a shrug. "When the doctor comes this afternoon, he may decide to let you go. Meanwhile, amuse yourself. There's television, games, and even a tape player if you care for golden oldies."

The man paced the floor for a while, not speaking to anyone, then wandered over to the old stereo system and looked through the stack of cassette tapes. He loaded one and pushed play.

The strains of Floyd Cramer's rendition of "Last Dance" filled the air. Gaynel danced through the door at that moment, and as she passed him the truck driver stepped in and took her hand as if the movement had been choreographed. They waltzed gracefully across the room.

In a moment they were cheek to cheek, her feet on top of his as they moved in unison, eyes closed and both smiling. It looked like a scene from a high school dance in the fifties or sixties. The day room grew quiet as everyone sat entranced at what appeared to be a moment captured from an almost forgotten past.

As the last note played, they stepped apart. He bowed, and she curtsied. David Sage began to clap softly, and others joined him. The truck driver looked at the group, smiled, then bowed again at the waist, making a dapper sweeping movement with his hand.

"Peace to you, my child," Gaynel said, whirling away.

After lunch the truck driver was no longer with them. He had left the ward—cured by Gaynel of whatever had ailed him. Of that Sage was certain.

The rest of that day was one of peace for the depressed detective. The truck driver had been saved—and so would David Sage be saved. He had only to keep the faith.

∽

It was the dream again.

The red eyes glowed from the darkness on each side of David Sage as he walked slowly down the long, damp tunnel to the wooden door, waiting for whatever kind of creatures were behind the red eyes to lunge out of the darkness and grab him in slobbering jaws.

Opening the wooden door, with terror washing over him, he saw her, the angelic female, naked and standing with her right side to him.

She reached and took his hand, then turned to face him, exposing the shredded and mutilated side of her body, with snowy white bone and muscles and tendons writhing like a bag of snakes.

"*You would have been better off with a millstone around your neck,*" she hissed through the twisted, smiling lips. "*Come and love me.*" She pulled him toward her even as he struggled. The bloody, tattered mouth was about to meet his . . .

"David! David! Help me."

The voice was coming from far away, but it pulled him from the clutches of the mangled angelic female. Sage sat up, covered with cold sweat.

"David, help me!"

It was Edward's voice, but he was not in his bed. For a moment, Sage thought he was still dreaming.

"David, help!"

Squinting in the darkness, Sage saw that the double panes of safety glass were leaning against the wall by Edward's bed. He got up and padded across the room.

"Edward?"

"Down here . . . on the ledge."

Gingerly, Sage leaned out the window. Edward was looking up, terror and agony in his eyes. He was standing on the six-inch ledge.

"How long have you been out there?"

"It seems like *hours*. I couldn't wake you. Go get help!"

"Here, take my hand." Sage reached down.

"No, no! I'm too heavy for you. The ledge was farther down than I thought. Go get help! I feel like my legs are about to give out."

"All right."

The young night nurse glanced up, annoyed, as Sage approached the desk. She was engrossed in a Harlequin romance and the orderly was nowhere in sight.

"Yes?" she asked, raising her eyebrows.

"Edward has climbed out on the ledge and can't get back in the room. It was farther down than he thought it was."

"I beg your pardon?" She was a pretty woman with skin the color of ebony.

"Edward took the window out and climbed out on the ledge. I don't know how long he's been out there, but I think you'd better call for help."

"Oh, my God!" She ran down the hall to the room. A moment later she emerged, a look of panic on her face.

"He's out on the ledge!" she almost screamed.

"I know. You'd better call hospital security. Have them get the fire department over here with a net in case he falls before they can get him down."

"Right. That's what I'll do." She frantically began to punch the number for Security.

Sage went back to the room and leaned out the window. "Help's on the way, Edward."

"Thanks. What time is it?"

He looked at his watch. "One-thirty."

"I've been out here an hour and a half. Why wouldn't you wake up? I screamed myself hoarse." His tone had an accusatory ring to it.

"I asked for a sleeping pill last night. I've been having a nightmare, but it didn't help."

"Well, thanks a hell of a lot for telling me!"

"I didn't know you were going to climb out on the ledge." Sage was becoming amused at Edward's precarious situation.

"If I'd told you, you'd have snitched me out."

A beam of light hit Edward from below. In the light from the parking lot, Sage saw two security officers, apparently checking to see if there really was someone on the ledge.

The ward door opened and Sage heard strange voices. The night nurse came in, followed by two more security officers.

"Mr. Sage," she said, "I appreciate your alerting me. But please go down to the day room while we get Edward inside."

"Sure."

He walked barefoot to the day room because he had left his house shoes by the bed. There was fresh coffee, even at one-thirty in the morning. He found a cinnamon roll with Katrina's name on it in the refrigerator. He knew she wouldn't eat it anyway.

As he sat munching the roll, Gaynel danced through the door and began to whirl in wide circles across the polished tile floor amid the chrome and plastic chairs, by the Ping-Pong table. Sage did not try to talk to her. He felt no need to do so. In due time she would save him, give him back his soul. He was convinced of that, and it was not his to know the day or the hour. It was only his to keep the faith.

❦

"Edward, why did you climb out on the ledge last night? I was about to discharge you." Dr. Wohlford was clearly put out with Edward.

"The voices, Doc. The voices told me to do it."

"Edward, you are *not* manifesting any other symptoms whatsoever of schizophrenia, except for the alleged voices. You can't stay in this ward forever. You have to face the world again." The doctor's Adam's apple was bobbing vigorously over a plum-colored bow tie.

"But I *want* to be cured. I want the voices to go away. I *really* do," the tall, lanky, pretend hippie said plaintively.

"Seven more days and that's it." Dr. Wohlford made a notation on his pad and moved over to Sage's table. Edward smiled in relief. His agony on the ledge had bought him another week in a lock-up ward.

"How are you feeling, David?" He flipped through until he came to Sage's chart. Without waiting for an answer, he went on. "Is the new medication helping yet?"

"I really can't tell any difference."

"Are you still seeing the savior?"

"Yes. The savior was here in this day room a little before two this morning."

"David, did you have imaginary friends as a boy?"

"Yes, but nothing like this. The savior is *real* to me."

"Do you have conversations with him?"

"Not really." Sage did not correct him as to gender. "Sometimes the savior speaks to me, though."

"All right. I'm going to leave you on the same medication for a while. Maybe we'll get some positive results this week. I'll be out of town for a few days, beginning tomorrow. Dr.

Wilson will be seeing my patients while I'm gone."

"He won't try to give me electroconvulsive therapy will he?" Sage half joked.

"Of course not. After all, you signed yourself in here. Nothing can be done without your consent."

He moved his tall, lanky frame over to the couch where Gaynel was sitting, head back and eyes closed. Before he could speak, though, she got up and whirled away. He shook his head, made a note on the clipboard, then left.

"Damn it, Gaynel, you're gonna have to try harder! Maybe you *needed* a rest, but you've had it now. It's time to come home!"

"I know. I know." Gaynel cringed back against the arm of the old leather couch, fear in her eyes.

"You *do* still love our children, don't you?" George Potts was wearing a Western-style string tie. Wearing any kind of tie was obviously a rare occasion for him. A roll of fat spilled out over his collar. A turquoise and silver slide held the tie together.

"Of course I do. Of course I do. And I try. I really *try*," Gaynel said in a singsong voice as she rocked back and forth.

"Well, you're not tryin' hard enough!" His voice rose in pitch. "I'm just about at the end of my rope, I can tell you that!"

As usual, Sage was sitting at a table nearby, just in case he was needed. It was all he could do to restrain himself when Gaynel's husband came and drove the savior into hiding. The man had lived with Gaynel, even had children with her, but was obviously unworthy of her.

That night Sage's dilemma was solved by Clifford

Bigman. He had been stalking around ever since he had awakened from the shot they had given him in the emergency room, not bothering anyone, just glaring at the world through his pale amber eyes.

For some reason, he had fixed on Gaynel's husband, the big, beefy-looking man in cowboy boots. Clifford never told anybody why. It was certainly not Gaynel's welfare that drew him to the old leather couch. Perhaps the man reminded him of someone else. Clifford puffed on his cigarette to get the tip really hot, then stepped in and pushed the fire against the left cheek of Gaynel's husband, grinding it in.

For a moment it was as if the big man didn't feel anything, then suddenly he jerked away, slapping at his face. "You black sonofabitch!" he screamed.

"Don't call me names, you white motherfucker!" Clifford Bigman yelled back. "I don't take shit from peckerwoods!"

Two orderlies started toward Clifford. "Get us some help!" one of them yelled to the nurse.

"Beal on deck! Beal on deck!" The old sailor laughed.

"Has anybody seen my wife?" Mr. Yow screamed.

Gaynel got up and danced out of the day room, unnoticed by her burly husband who was scuffling with Clifford. "I'll tear your fuckin' head off, nigger!"

"Nigger? You're callin' me a nigger now, you redneck bastard?" Clifford was advancing when the two orderlies grabbed him—one pinning his arms behind him, while the other applied a headlock.

"Let go of me!" Clifford screamed as they went to the floor. Sage was tempted from habit to jump in, but restrained himself. His jurisdiction was outside in the real world.

"You're damn lucky," Gaynel's husband snarled as the evening nurse led him by the arm toward the day room door.

"I eat punks like you for breakfast!"

"Oh yeah? Well eat my *dick*!" Clifford screamed from the writhing pile of bodies on the floor.

George Potts pretended that he was trying to get loose from the nurse, but Sage knew he really didn't want to. It was simple primate posturing. In a moment the nurse had walked him away, explaining that Clifford was a sick man and that she would explain to Gaynel why he had cut the visit short—as if Gaynel even cared that he had left.

"This is quite a place, Dave. How much are they charging you for the privilege of staying here?"

"I don't know. The insurance pays most of it. How did you know where to find me?" Sage looked up and smiled at his partner, Larry Ware, who had approached without being noticed.

"I'm a cop, remember?" He sat down in one of the folding chairs brought in for visitors. "Besides, Jamey Olivia called and told me where you were. I meant to get here last night, but I got tied up.

"What was *that* all about?" He nodded toward the dispute in progress and toward Mr. Beal and Mr. Yow who were still screaming out periodically.

"The black guy on the floor burned a big redneck visitor with a cigarette, but the nurse got the redneck out before he could hurt the black guy," Sage replied contemptuously.

"I take it you don't like the redneck?" Larry lit an unfiltered Pall Mall, the overhead lights reflecting off the nickel-plated Zippo lighter he always carried.

"Nope, and I don't like the black guy, either. The redneck's scared, and the black guy's glad of it, I think."

"Can't you get along with your fellow human beings, even in this asylum?" Larry laughed. Then his voice became serious. "As a matter of information, you be careful with the black kid.

He's a sick and dangerous motherfucker. You won't believe why he's here."

"He looks like the kind who would try to rape his mother. It's something in his eyes," David Sage said. "Besides, the monkey house switchboard is even faster than the police grapevine."

"Smartass." Ware chuckled affectionately.

"Does anyone else know I'm in the psych ward?" Sage asked his partner.

"You mean, does Lieutenant 'Lardass' Bullock know you're here? The answer is no. He was bitching about your absences again this morning, but I told him you were having kidney problems."

"Why kidney problems? Why not a bad liver or a brain tumor?"

"It was the first thing that came to my mind. I don't think there's any danger that he'll come and visit you."

"Thanks." Sage lit a cigarette. "What else is going on?"

"You know better than me. The court of appeals threw out Lyda Herrel's conviction on the grounds that the trial judge erred by not allowing testimony about her childhood problems. She's being released, pending a new trial."

"What's different about that?" Sage shrugged.

"This is your *partner* you're talking to. You wanted to shoot the bitch, and rightly so. And then, after what *she* had done, her parents tried to get you fired."

"Yeah, well things look different when you're being investigated by IA. After the review board cleared me, I quit thinking about it. Let sleeping dogs lie. It's all in the past, Larry."

"You can fool everybody else, but not me. I know what it did to you—what it's still doing to you. What I want to know is, are you thinking about killing her again? Is that why you've got yourself locked up?"

"Lyda doesn't mean jack-shit to me anymore! *All right, Larry?*"

"Sure, sure." Larry raised his hands, pale palms forward. "Forget I mentioned it."

"Sorry. I didn't mean to snap at you. It was a rough case, and I took a lot of flack over it, but it's finished. Lyda Herrel's attorney has done what we knew he would do, and there's nothing either of us can do about it."

"We both know she wasn't insane," Larry said, his dark face wrinkling in disgust. "She's just plain *evil*."

"Yeah, but *evil's* not a legal term, is it?" Sage asked.

"Nope, and we're not priests, are we?" Larry slapped his hand down on the table and changed the subject. "When will you be out of here? It's lonesome without a partner."

"I don't know." Sage put out his cigarette. "Soon, I hope."

"Well, keep me posted. I've gotta go. I've been at it for almost two days. I need some sleep." He got up and pushed his chair under the table.

"Thanks for coming."

They shook hands and the black detective walked away. Sage watched him leave, then shook out another cigarette and lit it with shaking hands.

"*That bitch, Lyda Herrel,*" he muttered under his breath, his fists clenched painfully. "That lousy, stinking, *evil* bitch! They should have drowned her when she was born." There are some things cops understand. What Lyda Herrel had done, though, was beyond comprehension, outside the pale of human culture. To make matters worse, it had been Christmas morning when the young patrolman called David Sage to the hospital . . .

"I hated to call you out on Christmas Eve, Sergeant Sage, but I just didn't quite know how to handle this. Hell, I don't even know how to classify it." The patrol officer looked like a kid. *They looked younger all the time.*

"Any time you're not sure, you call," Sage said with a yawn. That seemed to put him at ease. It was Sage's weekend on call, three in the morning. Whatever cropped up as a major crime, or one that patrol couldn't classify, was his.

It didn't matter, though. He had been by to see his daughter, Rita, and to drop off presents, at his ex-wife's new apartment. He really had nothing else to do with his time. The young patrol officer had called him to the hospital, interrupting his first attempted night's sleep of the weekend. "Just fill me in," Sage told him.

"Got a woman in here who showed up with some vaginal bleeding. She told the doctor that she'd miscarried. The doctor says she's given birth to a full-term baby."

"He's sure?"

"Says he is. She flatly denies it, though."

"You did the right thing by calling, Officer . . ." Sage looked at his name tag. ". . .Walker. I'll see if I can get to the bottom of it."

The young patrol officer left, elated that he had done the right thing and relieved that it had been taken out of his hands.

The night clerk looked up and smiled as the automatic doors whooshed loudly. Without asking, she poured the detective a cup of coffee. She handed him the Styrofoam cup.

"Dark and strong," the young black woman said, "just the way you like your women." She winked lasciviously. They went back a long way; both were people of the night.

"You're not supposed to tell everybody," he responded.

"Just the *Horton Sentinel* and two television stations," she replied, hitting the security button to let him inside the emergency room.

The resident on duty, a tired young man with premature lines around his eyes and old-fashioned steel rimmed glasses, glanced up from a chart as Sage entered, wearing no coat or tie—in direct violation of departmental regulations. Some doctors don't like cops in their emergency room. Sage could always tell who they are, though. This one wasn't among that group.

"Tell me a story, Doc." Sage sat down in a padded chair behind the nurses' station.

"I've got a white female in trauma room two. She's thirty years old, not a young girl, and she's given birth within the last few hours. She claims to have miscarried. It's just not so."

"You're positive?"

"Not a doubt in my mind. I've got tearing and trauma. She claims she was throwing up and felt a burning sensation in her rectal area. Says that's what caused the tearing."

"Possible?" The detective took a sip of the strong black coffee.

"Anything's possible." He shrugged. "But I'm telling you there's a newborn out there somewhere—alive or dead. She gave birth in the last few hours. I've seen hundreds of deliveries."

"I'll talk to her." Sage got up to leave.

"She ain't right in the head," the young doctor told him.

Sage turned, a look of surprise on his face. "That's not a very scientific term, Doc."

"I'm not a psychiatrist. If I were, I'd call the woman a detached personality or a sociopath. I was raised in East

Tennessee, though, so I'll just tell you as one hillbilly to another. She ain't right in the head."

"What's her name?" Sage asked, finishing the coffee.

"Lyda Herrel."

The doctor's description was an understatement. Angry eyes peered at Sage from deep sockets buried in stark white flesh. The woman was morbidly and grossly fat. Flesh hung canopy-like over her forearms and knees and rolled several times around her neck. It was the eyes that caught Sage's attention, though, smoldering like coals buried in the white ash of a wood fire.

"Miss Herrel, I'm Detective David Sage—"

"Mizz Herrel," she snapped.

"Ms. Herrel . . . ," he started again.

"A *Miss* is a child who belongs to her father. I am a woman and I belong to *myself*."

"The doctor says you gave birth in the last few hours, *Mizz* Herrel. He says he's sure. I'd like to know where the baby is."

"The doctor don't know what he's talkin' about. I had a miscarriage."

"What did you do with the fetal material if you had a miscarriage?"

"I *flushed* it the same way I'd flush its father if I could get my hands on him. That black sonofabitch made *promises* to me, then left me high and dry."

"You miscarried while you were on the commode and you just *flushed* it away?"

"That's right." She shifted her enormous buttocks, which, because of the open back of her gown, were in direct contact with the plastic-covered examining table, making an ear-piercing squeaking sound as flesh stuck to plastic. "What else was I supposed to do with it?" Her voice was defiant.

"Ms. Herrel"—he removed a small notebook from his hip pocket—"if you don't cooperate with me . . ."

"Not *if*"—her eyes bored into his—"I *ain't* goin' to cooperate. I don't have to."

She was right. Sage left the room, walking past the doctor who had been listening in. The resident followed him through the security doors, out to the desk. The clerk handed Sage another cup of coffee.

"What will you do?" the doctor asked.

"If she lives with anyone, I'll go interview them."

"What if they can't tell you anything? A woman her size could go full-term without anyone noticing."

"Who are they, Doc?"

"Sorry. I forgot that you didn't know. Give the officer a copy of the information she gave when she came in," the young doctor told the ward clerk. "Her parents," he continued. "She says she lives with her parents and also works for them."

"That doesn't sound much like a liberated woman. She made a big deal of being called Ms. instead of Miss."

"I told you that she ain't right in the head, didn't I?"

"Yeah, you did." The detective looked at the sheet the clerk had handed him with a sinking sensation. The address was all the way out at the northeast end of the county, in Shagbark. He knew he wouldn't sleep again that Christmas Day.

"She says that she's a dog handler," the clerk giggled. "She must get along well with the rest of the bitches."

"Now, now, Tabitha." Sage reached out and patted her hand. "You mustn't be so judgmental. You'll start sounding like a cop if you aren't careful."

"You haven't answered my question," the young doctor

said, massaging the bridge of his nose. "What if they corroborate her story?"

"Doctor, I'll do the best I can. It's not a simple matter. We cops labor under a thing called the U.S. Constitution. I'll just have to play it by ear."

"I know," the young doctor said tiredly. "We all have rules to live by. I'm going to keep her here as long as I can. That'll at least give you time to investigate before she goes home."

"That will work," Sage told him. "I'm going out to wake up her parents now."

"She probably had a litter and sold it," the ward clerk said as the detective turned to leave. "I bet her puppies look like those really wrinkled Chinese dogs."

"'Bye, Tabitha. Try to be good," Sage said over his shoulder.

It was a twenty-five-minute drive to the address Lyda Herrel had given. Sage had no trouble finding it, even in the dark. A big white sign proclaimed: HERREL FARMS, BLACK ANGUS CATTLE. Then in smaller letters, obviously added later because the paint was brighter, "Award Winning Rottweilers."

He walked across the front yard, half expecting large black-and-tan dogs to come hurtling out of the darkness, but there was no sound. Apparently the animals were kept somewhere away from the house.

The man who answered Sage's knock was slight with wisps of white hair standing in all directions. Behind him, Sage could see a scraggly cedar tree, probably cut from somewhere off his farm. It was roped with popcorn and other homemade ornaments. The man peered at the detective suspiciously.

"Detective David Sage, Horton County Sheriff's Department." He held his star up at eye level. "I need to come in and ask you and your wife some questions?"

"About what? This ain't a good time to wake up a farmer. The cattle has to be fed at daybreak."

"About your daughter," the detective answered.

"She ain't been hurt, has she?" A look of alarm came over his face.

"Lyda is all right, but I need to talk to you and your wife."

"Can't it wait 'til mornin'?"

"No, sir. I wouldn't be here in the middle of the night if I didn't think it was important."

"Oh, all right." He jerked the door open and stepped aside. An obscenely fat woman with iron-gray hair waddled into the living room in a ragged flannel gown. After seeing her mother, Sage wondered briefly if Lyda Herrel's weight problem was due to some kind of hereditary glandular condition.

"What is it, Rafe?" She rubbed at her eyes.

"This here is a county detective. He wants to ask us some questions about Lyda."

"Is Lyda in trouble?" the woman asked, her eyes coming fully open.

"Not exactly. Would the two of you sit down? I'll be as brief as possible."

They perched on the edge of a love seat, the woman's gigantic rear end taking up more than half of it. For a moment Sage had a brief mental picture of the boney little man trying to copulate with the elephantine woman. They stared at him questioningly.

"Your daughter is at Saint Elizabeth's Hospital. She says she's had a miscarriage. The emergency room resident says she has delivered a full-term baby in the last few hours."

"I knowed it!" the woman blurted out. "I knowed there

was somethin' goin' on between her and that nigger, Elgin Mattress! You wouldn't listen, though, would you?" Her porcine eyes glittered the way her daughter's eyes had glittered earlier at the hospital. The little man seemed to shrivel under her glare.

"We needed him," he said apologetically, glancing at the floor. "Help is hard to come by for what we can afford to pay."

"Yeah, and now he's shamed our daughter," the woman said bitterly. "Not just a bastard, but a little *black* bastard."

"Who are you talking about?" Sage asked.

"Elgin Mattress," the man said. "He was our hired hand until a few weeks ago."

Sage jotted the name down. "Where is Mr. Mattress now?"

"He's gone far away, I'd guess," the woman shrilled. "He's got my little girl in trouble, and now he's run off to evade his part in it."

"Have you noticed anything unusual about Lyda the last few weeks? The doctor says he's *sure* she delivered a full-term baby. She's a pretty heavy girl. Do you think . . ."

"She ain't *that* heavy," the woman growled. "I'd a noticed it if she was ready to have a baby." Suddenly, there was hope on the woman's face. "Of course, if she *says* she ain't had a baby, then she ain't had a baby. *That's* the end of it."

"Would you mind if I looked around, especially in Lyda's room?"

"I don't see why not—" the man began.

"Yeah, we do mind," the woman said sharply, silencing her husband. "You ain't got a search warrant, have you? And we ain't done nothin' wrong. You can't just walk in here and search a person's house. We got rights!"

"Sometimes young women who deliver babies experience a form of shock, Mrs. Herrel," Sage said as diplomatically as possible. "I don't mean to intrude on your privacy, but I really do need to look around."

"We've answered your questions," she said, leaning forward. "You can leave now, or I'll call the sheriff's department."

For a few moments Sage sat quietly. He knew he was on shaky legal ground. Had he been sure of the existence of an infant, he would have searched the house and the law be damned. But he wasn't sure, despite what the doctor had said.

How could Lyda Herrel's parents not have noticed that she was full-term, about to deliver? Maybe grossly fat women have physical peculiarities with which the doctor was not familiar. A cop doesn't violate the sanctity of a person's home, at least not lightly. Sergeant David Sage, at that moment, made what was perhaps the worse decision of his career, as far as he was concerned anyway.

"All right." He handed the man one of his cards. "If you have anything further to tell me after Lyda gets home tomorrow, you can call me at this number, or page me directly at this number." Mrs. Herrel was staring at Sage, a look of triumph on her cartoon-like face as he stood to leave.

Later, he would go over the incident a thousand times in his mind. Sometimes he cleared himself of negligence, just as a review board would eventually clear him. At other times, he felt he couldn't live with the decision he had made. To make matters worse, the new dream had started, robbing him of whatever rest he previously had managed to snatch here and there.

That's the way with most momentous events, though. They don't seem momentous at the time.

EIGHT

"How long have you been a practicing homosexual?" Nurse Grady asked. She had a piece of bacon caught between her enormous front teeth, but no one in the group had told her.

"He ain't *practicin'*," Clifford Bigman interrupted. "I bet he got it down pat."

Nurse Grady glared at Clifford but said nothing. The aging law student answered as if the big man had not interjected. He had heard the joke before.

"Since I was about fourteen years old." Raymond paused to light one of the long, thin cigarettes. "I don't think I'm *basically* homosexual. I believe it's just learned behavior that I can stop with a little help."

Clifford Bigman snorted contemptuously and folded his arms, but said nothing. He had spent another night in restraints after grinding out the cigarette on Mr. Potts's face. Nurse Grady looked at him but did not invite comment.

"How did it come about, Raymond?" Nurse Grady asked.

"Well, I was always a sickly, weak child. Some boys cornered me in the locker room when I was in the ninth grade. They made me . . . forced me . . . you know . . . to perform oral sex. I didn't want to, but I was afraid. . . ."

"Crap!" Clifford Bigman unfolded his arms and sat up in the folding chair. "No *normal* boy would have give in. You were born a faggot and the rest of the boys just took advantage of it."

"Sound's like you're speaking from experience, Clifford," Sage said quietly.

"What?" He jumped to his feet. "Who the hell do you think you're talkin' to, peckerwood?"

"Sit down, Clifford. If you don't want the heat, then don't hand it out," the detective answered.

"That's right, Clifford, *sit down!*" There was iron in Nurse Grady's voice. He stood for a moment, nostrils heaving, then took his seat, apparently remembering the restraints.

"You're gonna push me too far, peckerwood," Clifford said to Sage. "When you do, I'm gonna hurt your white ass."

"I never pay attention to barking dogs, son. I've walked over better men than you to get to a *real* fight." Sage was embarrassed, even as he played the macho game, but something about Clifford Bigman really grated on his nerves. It had to do with the emotionless eyes and the boiling anger.

"That will be enough," Nurse Grady said. "You're both talking like children."

Before Clifford could say anything else, Katrina, fidgeting in her seat and twisting one of her perpetual lavender scarves, spoke. "Have you had any success in changing, Raymond?"

"Yes . . . I went six months, staying away from the gay community. I was dating a woman regularly and we were on the verge of a sexual relationship. Then . . . I ended up back here again with an overdose of sleeping pills."

"What happened, Raymond?" Sage asked.

"An old acquaintance showed up. He wanted me to . . . you know."

"Give him a blow job?" Clifford snickered.

"Yes! *That's* what he wanted. I told him no, but he began threatening me. He's big. I tried to resist, but he wouldn't leave me alone. I gave in . . . and after he left, I took the pills."

"Ain't no real man in the world gonna do *that* to another man," Clifford told Raymond. "You *like* it and just don't want to admit that you do."

"That's not true," Raymond sobbed. "I *don't* like it, I'm just afraid."

"I think Raymond has had a good session," Nurse Grady told the group. "Let's let him rest. Katrina, are you gaining any weight?"

The nurse very well knew the answer when she asked the question. Twice a day the orderlies and aides weighed all patients, took their blood pressure, and asked if their bowels had moved.

"No. I've lost another pound."

"Do you know why you're having trouble eating, Katrina?"

"I'm just not hungry. All I can think of is going back to work."

"How long have you been off now?" Mr. Yow asked, startling the rest of them with his coherency.

"Three months, but my boss told me my job would be waiting when I got back."

"Have you called him during the three months?" Nurse Grady asked.

"No."

"Why not?"

"I don't know." Silence fell over the group.

"Katrina's finished, I think. Gaynel. Gaynel! Open your eyes. How do you feel about what Raymond and Katrina had to say this morning?"

"I'm sorry, child"—she peered at Nurse Grady through the

thick, distorting lenses—"but I wasn't here. My spirit was roaming this morning in the celestial realm."

"No, Gaynel. Your spirit was here, but your *mind* was wandering. You have to face whatever sent you here."

Silence fell once more. Gaynel merely smiled at Nurse Grady, the type of smile reserved for children. The nurse turned her attention to David Sage.

"How long have you been a police officer, David?"

"Fifteen years."

"Did you always want to be a police officer?"

"No, I wanted to teach English literature and write poetry. I applied for a job with the sheriff's department after I flunked out of college."

"Did you like it right away?" Raymond asked.

"No, but for the first time in my life I felt like I was doing something worthwhile. Lately, I'm not sure, though."

"Is that because you fucked up a case, or did you git somebody killed?" The pain went briefly through the police officer's eyes. Bigman's face lit up as he realized that he had hit a nerve. "I got a thang about people. I *understand* men and women, *Mr. Poleeceman.* So answer my question. What did you do that was so bad that you couldn't live with it?" Clifford was savoring the moment. For the first time Sage realized that the young man looked a lot like the late Nat King Cole.

"I was brought up on departmental charges, but I was exonerated."

"Exonerated of what?" Edward leaned in, waiting for the officer's answer.

"I was accused of dereliction of duty and contributing to a wrongful death, but I was cleared."

"I say where there's smoke there's fire," the young black man said. "I bet you were *suspended.*"

"Then exonerated and given back pay!" Sage replied, more defensively than he had intended.

"Would you like to tell us about the accusations?" Nurse Grady asked.

"A woman by the name of Lyda Herrel showed up at a hospital claiming that she had just miscarried," Sage told the group. "The emergency room doctor called the sheriff's department. He thought she had not miscarried, but had given birth. I was sent out to investigate. She continued to deny having given birth, so I went to the farm where she lived with her parents.

"The parents claimed that they knew of no pregnancy, and as it turned out they were telling the truth. Lyda was extremely overweight and they just hadn't been able to tell. The doctor was right, though. She *had* given birth and the baby died."

"Why didn't you search the house?" Raymond asked, leaning forward.

"Because I didn't feel at the time that I had enough probable cause to intrude on Lyda's parents. I didn't have any concrete evidence that she had delivered a baby, and if she had, there was a chance it had happened somewhere else."

"Was the baby in the house at the time you questioned the parents?" Edward asked.

"Yes. If I had made the search, the baby probably would have survived. It was a judgement call, though. That's why I was exonerated by the review board."

"Was that when you began to abuse drugs and alcohol?" Raymond asked.

"No. That didn't really start until about six months ago," Sage replied.

"All right, David," Nurse Grady said quietly. "That was a good, honest exchange." Her look told David Sage that she thought she had stumbled upon a major clue to his problems and had decided to let it emerge slowly. Sage had always been of the opinion that all mental health workers are simplistic.

"Mr. Beal, do you have anything to add today?" the nurse inquired. To their surprise, the old sailor answered. They all slowly turned to listen.

"I was on the USS *Indianapolis*," he said with a toothless grin. "She went down and nobody knowed where we was. The sharks et a bunch of sailors that night. The devils would come up and drag people out of the boats. It was the largest shark feast in history."

"Does that still bother you?" Nurse Grady asked, a look of interest on her horsey face.

"Does what still bother me?"

"Having watched your friends eaten alive by sharks. Does it still bother you?"

"No." He smiled again, showing pink gums.

"Then why did you bring it up?" Edward asked.

"Bring what up?" the old sailor asked guilelessly.

"You said the sharks ate a lot of sailors," Edward said, his voice rising in irritation.

"That's right," Mr. Beal answered. "That was when the USS *Indianapolis* was sunk by the Japs. Nobody knowed where we was."

"Will you answer the question?" Edward asked, clearly annoyed.

"Beal on deck! Beal on deck!" the old sailor began to yell, gone from the day-to-day world again, leaving the questions unanswered. The orderly led him off to the day room.

"Edward, would you like to share with us today?" the nurse asked.

"Yeah. I'd like to talk about the voices. I've identified one.

It's the voice of an Apache warrior."

"Does he speak in the Apache language?" Sage asked.

"Well, he probably does, but I *hear* him in English."

"Maybe you're not crazy at all. Maybe you're a psychic channeler," the detective told him. "In that case you can get out of here and make a lot of bucks telling fortunes."

"We don't use the word *crazy* in here, David," Nurse Grady told him in ominous tones.

"I'm sure it's not *real*," Edward sounded alarmed. "It's all a figment of my imagination. I'm schizophrenic."

"We don't toss around diagnostic terms, either, Edward. None of us here are doctors," the nurse reminded him.

Without warning, the ward door just outside the meeting room opened and the air was filled with feminine screeching and cursing.

"You cocksuckers had better let go of me! I'll have a writ of habeas corpus before it gets dark. Bastards! I was minding my own business, trying to see the dean of law!"

Her voice faded as the orderlies fought her past the door and down the hallway to a room.

"Dr. Hart is back," Raymond said with an emphatic nod.

"It would appear so," Nurse Grady sighed.

"Who is Dr. Hart?" Sage asked.

"She's a law professor. She was in and out of here ten days ago. Talk about *crazy*," Edward said. "She's a manic depressive who makes everyone here, including Mr. Beal, look *normal*."

Nurse Grady did not correct him.

The man was in the day room sitting in one of the plastic and chrome chairs when they returned from group therapy. His face was an enormous, purplish blob of scar tissue with a car-icature of human features roughly molded into it. He looked like a partially melted wax statue. The scarring extended halfway back on his scalp; lank gray hair hung straight to his shoulders beyond the scar tissue, like the hair on a rubber Halloween mask.

Swaggering into the day room, Clifford Bigman didn't see him until he spoke.

"Excuse me, Lieutenant Jeeter, I need to speak to you about my check," the scarred man said. The tall black youth turned his eyes to the man, a sarcastic answer on his lips. His amber eyes opened wide, and he recoiled from the apparition, falling over another chair in his haste to put space between them.

"What the hell is this," Bigman stammered, "*Halloween?* We shouldn't have to look at—"

The man got up and walked toward Clifford with his hand extended as if reaching for help. "Lieutenant Jeeter, if you'll just check for me—"

"GET THE HELL AWAY FROM ME! *Get him away from me!*" Clifford turned and ran from the day room. An orderly intercepted the man with the melted face and led him back to a chair.

"Sit down, Gordon. I'll bring you a snack," the orderly told him soothingly.

"That *was* Lieutenant Jeeter, wasn't it? I just wanted him to give me a little help. I didn't mean to upset him, being new in the unit and all."

"No, Gordon, that wasn't Lieutenant Jeeter and you're not in the army anymore."

"That's ridiculous," the man said through lips that were stretched and purple. "Of course, I'm in the army. I just landed in Saigon two days ago. I'm really looking forward to combat. It's a family tradition, you know."

"Whatever you say, Gordon. Just don't bother that man anymore. He's not a friendly soul," the orderly said.

"Well then, would you point out the financial officer for me? I really need to straighten things out."

"Later, Gordon. For now just sit and be quiet." The scarred man leaned back in his chair with a sigh and sat quietly.

"It looks like Clifford Bigman has found someone who frightens him," David Sage said to Edward.

"Yeah, but he won't be here long. Gordon's almost a permanent resident at the Veteran's Administration Hospital at Murfreesboro. They let him out for a few days, then he's back here in a week or so, thinking it's the sixties again."

"Men like him are one of the tragedies of combat." Sage paused to light a cigarette. "They go to war idealistic and ready to die for their country, then some of them come back like him, scarred for life."

"That didn't happen in combat," Edward replied. "Gordon Platt was in the army all right, but when they gave him his orders for Vietnam, he poured gasoline over himself and lit it."

"He did *that* to *himself*?" Sage asked, horrified.

"Yes. His father's retired military. Highly decorated, I understand. Lives in Horton. Sometimes he visits Gordon when he's here between trips to the VA hospital. Silver-haired guy. He sits with tears in his eyes while Gordon talks as if he's still in the army and it's 1968."

As they were discussing him, Gordon got up and walked to their table. "Excuse me, Sergeant Clark," he said to David Sage, "but isn't Lieutenant Jeeter still the executive officer?"

"I really don't know, Soldier," Sage answered, almost recoiling inwardly. A man with such tragedy thrust upon him can be pitied; a man who has done such a thing to himself is merely frightening.

"I really need to find the financial officer. My check's been screwed up for months."

Visiting hours were over. There had been no one to see Sage, which wasn't surprising since only Jamey and his partner knew where he was. Larry had phoned, though, to see if he needed anything. Gaynel was at the back of the day room, dancing in swirls and pirouettes, eyes closed. Edward and Raymond were finishing a game of chess, and the catatonic fifteen-year-old, Rachel, was sitting at a table, hands folded in front of her. A bored orderly with a greasy blond ponytail sat reading a newspaper, waiting for shift change. Otherwise, the day room was deserted.

Sage's eyes fell on the girl, and he found himself looking her directly in the eyes. She smiled the kind of smile that you only see on the face of a baby, and he responded in kind, feeling a sort of elation. She was coming out of whatever private hell had sucked her in. She had not spoken, but her eyes had begun to follow people around the room.

Sage was about to speak to her when Clifford Bigman strode into the room. He paused, apparently looking to see if the scarred man was still up. Annoyed, David Sage looked to see if the orderly had noticed, but he had not looked up from his paper.

Bigman stood by the door, his feral eyes taking in everything with obvious contempt. He went to the refrigerator and rummaged through it, disregarding the names penned on each item until he found a carton of chocolate milk. He opened it, swallowed half, then walked over and sat down at Rachel's table.

"Want some chocklit milk, Sweet Cheeks?"

Her eyes focused on him for a moment, then moved on as if he were not there. He leaned in closer.

"You can *pretend* if you want, but ol' Clifford knows that you're really awake. Why don't you talk to me? We could get to be *real* close. You're a pretty little thing." He took another sip of the milk, leaving a ring over his upper lip.

"Still don't wanna talk, huh. Maybe I just need to get your attention. What if I just take a little look at your titties?"

He reached over and lifted her shirt. She was wearing no bra. Clifford put his hand over a cupcake-size breast, then pinched a pink nipple. Her eyes did not even flutter. For a moment Sage sat shocked, unable to believe what Bigman had done. It was like molesting a baby. The police officer in Sage took over without conscious thought; he moved quickly and silently.

"Whooeee! Feel that nipple," Clifford said. "You like that, don't you, Sweet Cheeks. I . . . ahhhhhhh!"

David Sage had locked onto Clifford's hand with what cops call a "come-a-long" hold, with the palm inward and upward. The slightest movement from Sage induced intense pain. A hundred-pound woman can control an opponent twice her size if she knows a few simple moves. Sage guided the big man away from the table, then forced him to his knees.

"You're breakin' my wrist!" Clifford whined.

"If you ever touch this child again, I'll break your back!" Sage told him through clenched teeth.

"*Whoa*, Mr. Sage, what's the problem?" The orderly had appeared next to them but made no move to intervene.

"This scumbag was fondling Rachel." The orderly looked

at her where she sat with one breast still exposed. He reached over and pushed her blouse down.

"Let go, Mr. Sage. I'll handle it from here."

Sage turned loose and stepped back, nostrils still flaring in rage, ready for an attack. Clifford collapsed on the floor momentarily. *It always shocks the big ones*, Sage thought, *the ones used to using brute strength to get their way, when they meet opposition.*

"I'll get you for this!" Clifford growled, holding his hand to his chest. "You won't catch me off guard the next time!"

"It won't matter," Sage answered. "The end result will be the same. Don't touch this child again."

"Let's go, Clifford. It's time for bed," the orderly told him.

"I ain't ready for bed."

"It's a shot and bed—or you go into restraints," said the orderly, a psychology major working part-time at the hospital. "Doctor's orders."

"All right, I'll go. But you better watch out *Mr. Cop.* Nobody pushes Clifford Bigman around. Nobody!"

"Let's go, now," the orderly said.

"You're a policeman?"

For a moment Sage didn't realize where the voice was coming from. Then he looked down and saw Rachel staring up at him with eyes so wide that they looked as if they had been treated with belladonna.

"Yes, I am."

"Policemen help people, don't they?" Her sentences were rendered up like phrases from a baby, but she was talking!

"We try, Rachel. We really do."

That was all she said. A moment later she was gone from her body again.

∞

"Dave?"

"What, Edward?"

"You're smoking in bed again, aren't you?"

"Yes, I am."

"Does the doctor still buy your story that you've met the savior?"

"I have met the savior, Edward."

"Why does he believe you and not me?"

"I don't know, Edward."

"Maybe the doctor would believe I'm schizophrenic if I met the savior, too."

"I doubt it, Edward. You need to find a delusion of your own. They generally aren't shared."

"I guess you're right."

There was silence for a moment.

"Edward?"

"What?"

"How did you get the window out?"

"I can't tell you. I might need to do it again if nothing else works."

NINE

Sage lay listening to Edward's soft snoring, trying to remember how he had ended up on 6 North for the third time, or even once for that matter. Psychiatric wards were not a part of the culture in which he had evolved as a human being. His father had believed that all mental illness was demonic possession. Maybe he was right. Sage had never seen his father's theory disproved, and it was at least as feasible as some of the other chic therapies he had run across or read about through the years.

While he was in the army being examined for a security clearance, he had met a therapist who was of the opinion that all emotional problems were the direct result of fairy tales and lies told to children. He asked what Sage's favorite childhood story was, and when Sage said, "Jack the Giant Killer," the therapist yelled, "Aha! I knew it." He never did tell Sage what it was he knew, though.

Sage hadn't stayed with the psychologist very long, having soon afterward been pronounced sane enough to work as a courier of top-secret documents and material.

When the depression first hit him, nearly twenty years later, it was Jamey Olivia who had saved his life, not medicine, alcohol, or shrinks.

He had first met Jamie when they were taking a class together at Horton State Community College. He and his wife had just separated, and Sage was filling a little spare time with a course on the Georgian poets. One evening the instructor, an effeminate man in his fifties who fancied himself an Oscar Wilde look-alike, made the comment that Ernest Dowson was "the most minor of the minor poets."

It just so happened that Ernest Dowson was the only poet, living or dead, who had ever made David Sage cry. He told the instructor that even a minor poet among minor poets was several steps above an effete college instructor with a practiced lisp. In turn, the instructor suggested that Sage drop the class—right then.

As David Sage walked out, radiating contempt, Jamey had followed him. He had noticed her earlier, to be sure. Jamey Olivia was not a woman who could walk by any man—any heterosexual man—without being noticed. She was not beautiful, but men always remembered her as beautiful. Later in their relationship, Sage learned to think of her as sloe-eyed—almost but not quite oriental, the result of Slavic ancestry—with a mane of raven hair falling down her back. Her hips were just a bit wide for most tastes, but Sage liked sturdy women.

"He's a real jerk, isn't he? I was hoping someone would tell him off so I could drop the class gracefully," she told Sage, rapidly walking up behind him. Her accent was Boston; not upper-class Boston, but the streets of Roxbury.

"I'll not listen to any degrading comments about Ernest Dowson," Sage said. "He's the only poet who ever came close to being as depressed as I am right now."

"I've noticed that. In fact, I told Kevin that the most depressed man I've ever met was taking a class with me." She fell in step with him as they reached the parking lot. "I told him I was going to introduce myself to you."

"Who's Kevin?"

"My husband."

"Your husband doesn't object to your introducing yourself to strange men?"

"I suppose he does, but there isn't much he can do about it, except leave. And that he'll *never* do."

"I wouldn't put up with it."

"I know you wouldn't. You're a barbarian and a poet. I realized that the first time I saw you."

"I may well be a barbarian, but whether or not I'm a poet is debatable. Once I thought I was. Now, I don't know."

"Oh, you're a poet. Cop is written all over you, and only a poetic cop would be studying the Georgian poets. It's not in the criminal justice curriculum." She laughed a deep, pulsating, husky laughter.

He smiled at her in spite of himself.

"Let's go get a drink," she said.

"Where?" he asked. When she had approached, David Sage had been seriously considering going home and "eating his gun," a police euphemism for suicide. He thought her offer over and decided to go with her. The gun would always be available. As with Nietzsche, David Sage had been able to get through one dark day after another with the comforting thought that he could end the pain whenever he wished.

"Quincy's Piano Bar."

"Will they let a cop in such a chic place?"

"We'll tell them you're a scientist. They'll never know the difference. Follow me down there." She turned as if the matter had been decided and walked to her red BMW. Sage got into his battered old Ford Taurus and followed. Jamey had been right. The place was packed with pseudo-intellectuals and instructors from the university art staff. They were pretenders all. She introduced Sage as a molecular biologist working on the cloning of Cuban frogs. They had all nodded perkily, smiling and giving him limp-wristed handshakes between deep discussions of the latest trend in art.

"Go home with me," she said after an hour or so of having fun at the expense of the academics, men and women wrapped in advanced degrees and insulated from the real world.

"What about your husband?"

"He's out of town for the week."

"I don't know . . ."

"You *need* me tonight because you're a man on the brink of doing something horrible to himself. I have a fireplace and bearskin rug in my den. I want us to take our clothes off and wallow on that rug while you fuck me into a state of delirium. When we know each other better, you can make love to me. But for the time being, fucking is what you need."

She was right. He *had* needed her—more than he knew. Her arms and lips and warm wet places didn't cure his recurring dream, but they gave him something to look forward to. They pushed aside the terrible nightmares temporarily. When he slept with her, he seldom had the dream. Unfortunately, she had a husband who wanted to sleep with her most nights.

On many of those nights when she was sleeping with her husband, David Sage drank too much and took too many pills. Cops have no problem acquiring drugs once they pick up the habit. In his case, they came from a hero-worshiping pharmacist who was a member of the sheriff's auxiliary police unit. Every time he gave the detective another thirty tranquilizers, he'd admonish him about the dangers of drug addiction.

The first time David Sage ended up on the ward was after he passed out at a strip joint, a place he would never have entered in a sober condition—except in the line of duty. The manager was in a panic because he thought a cop was going to die on his premises.

The second time, he wrecked a car, ran it right into a divider wall on the interstate. A city patrol officer covered by sending him to the hospital before a supervisor could arrive. After doing a quick blood scan that revealed an incredibly high alcohol content, they had sent Sage right up to the psych ward.

This time Jamey had brought him in. David Sage was beginning to see how quickly a person could become institutionalized. No hassle, no worries. Just eat, sleep, and take drugs.

His physical salvation had come through a woman—the warmth and life flowing from Jamey Olivia as she absorbed his pain and anxiety. His spiritual salvation would come from Gaynel Potts, the savior, who was masquerading as a half-blind, frumpy housewife. He had only to await the right moment. He knew it was not for him to know the hour or the day.

"Time to wake up, Mr. Sage."

He opened his eyes and found the red-headed technician staring down at him. With a start, he realized that he had slept through the night without dreaming.

"You look different," he told her sleepily, sitting up in bed.

"I didn't think you'd notice." Her cheeks flushed and her hand fluttered up to her hair, which had been cut short, almost as short as Sage's, since the last time he'd seen her.

"Very attractive," he told her, meaning it and extending his arm.

"Thank you." She whipped the rubber cord around his muscular arm and tapped the inner elbow until a vein popped up.

"Tomorrow's Saturday. Are you going out on a pass?" She slid the needle into his arm, and crimson blood crept up into the clear tube past the little markings.

"I guess not."

"Your . . . your friend. She isn't coming this weekend?" The girl skillfully removed one tube and replaced it with another, drawing a second vial.

"She's out of town with her husband, and I don't have anyone else. Except for her and my partner, nobody else even knows I'm here."

"I could take you out." Her eyes were focused pointedly on her task, avoiding his gaze. "The afternoon shift people don't know me. I'd be in a lot of trouble if anyone found out I was dating a patient, but . . . You could say I'm your sister."

She let it hang.

For a minute he thought it over. He had heard one of the nurses tell Gaynel that she would be going for a weekend visit with her family.

"What would you like to do?" he asked.

"Whatever. A movie, lunch, a drive in the country."

"All right. I'll clear it with my doctor."

"Ten o'clock in the morning?"

"Sure."

"See you then." She became suddenly brisk and efficient again as she picked up her wire basket of samples. He watched her walk away. Looking at the vials of blood, Sage had wondered briefly if she handled the blood of AIDS patients, but didn't ask her.

∞

Dr. Chavez Wilson studied Sage with his deep-set, little eyes. They were set close together in a round face with the 1950s ducktail standing out from his head. At first glance, his eyes appeared crossed. Sage was going to miss the vacationing Dr. Wohlford, bow tie and all.

"So you want an overnight pass for this Saturday?"

"That's right."

"According to your file, you've never asked for a pass before. Why now?"

"Well, I thought I'd see if the savior would still appear to me outside the ward."

"You're not feeling suicidal are you?" The doctor looked at him suspiciously.

"No."

"Well . . . Dr. Wohlford didn't leave a note saying you *couldn't* have a pass, so I guess it's all right. Take Saturday night. If it goes well, we might try a whole weekend next time."

"Thanks."

"Does the medication seem to be helping?"

"I really can't tell much difference." Actually, there was no difference at all because Sage had been putting it under his tongue and flushing it down the toilet when nobody was looking. He was taking the tranquilizers, but not the drug that was supposed to alleviate his psychotic symptoms. *What if the drug destroyed his faith?*

"The nurse will fix you a packet of medicine. Don't forget to take it. It has a cumulative effect, you know."

"I'll be sure and take it."

Dr. Wilson made a quick notation and moved his Neanderthal-like body to the next table, where Edward the pseudo-hippy waited with a carefully rehearsed look of pain on his face.

"Well, Edward. How are you?" the psychiatrist asked.

"Not so good, Doc. The voices have turned into a chorus now. Like in the Bible. I think maybe I'm demon-possessed."

"Well, whatever," Dr. Wilson answered absent-mindedly, running his fingers through his ducktail on the right side. "When you leave, if you have any demons they can go with you."

"How come you people believe everyone else's fucking delusions and visions and not mine?" Edward demanded with a sulking look on his face.

"Because you're so transparent." The doctor made a notation on his chart and moved on to Gaynel's table.

She stood up and with a beatific smile on her face was about to dance away. "Sit down!" Dr. Wilson snapped. She complied but did not look at him.

"Gaynel, has the nurse explained that your husband is taking you home for the weekend?"

"I have no home in this earthly abode," she told him, looking across the aisle at Sage from the corner of her eye.

"We both know better than that, Gaynel. One day you will have to face the prospect of leaving here. You can lead a normal life if you'll continue to take your medication."

"May God bless your efforts," she said with a smile, then got up and danced away.

Dr. Chavez Wilson made a comment to himself about Gaynel's husband that Sage didn't quite catch, scratched a notation on the chart and went over to the old sailor, who was slumped forward in the wheelchair, a froth on his lips. He had just returned from his shock therapy. The old sailor would be like that for an hour or so, and would then wake up and once more begin to yell, "Beal on deck!" He had never explained to anyone where he thought he was when he cried out for himself.

Dr. Wilson opened one of the old man's eyes, then made another note on his pad as they wheeled Katrina in, slumped over and unconscious. Sage wondered what the doctor was looking for in the eyes of a patient driven unconscious by electricity that he himself had ordered to be charged through the delicate brain.

"You're actually going to do it, aren't you? You're going out with a *mental patient*," Sandra Carr said with a shake of her head. A tall, pale woman of twenty-three with her hair bobbed almost to the scalp, she presented a bold, striking figure and was never at a loss for a date, even on the spur of the moment.

"You *should* be proud of me," Lori Henderson said. "You're always complaining that I'm too meek and that I never go after what I want. Well, this time I did."

"For God's sake, Lori, I didn't mean some psychotic cop on mind-blowing, psychotropic drugs. There are thousands of perfectly acceptable men in this town who would be glad to take you out."

"Yeah, like Lewis Tryon. You were really sold on him. 'Money and breeding,' you said, but look what a totally selfish creep he turned out to be." *And*, Lori thought to herself, *a lover who left me totally unsatisfied night after night.*

"Besides," Lori went on, "I've had enough *boy*friends. I want a man this time, and I think I've found one."

"What's so great about him? He doesn't look all that handsome in that sheriff's department commemorative book picture. Where did you get it anyway?" Lori's roommate asked.

"I have a girlfriend from high school who works at the sheriff's department. She lent me the book and said if she'd known David Sage was single, she would have snapped him up herself. And get *this*, he has a medal of valor and two purple hearts for being wounded in the line of duty."

"So that's what you want, a macho cowboy, a wham-bam, thank you, ma'am?"

"He's not like that, Sandra."

"How would you know from just sticking a needle in his arm every morning?" Sandra asked.

"Here, read this. It's a short piece that David wrote for the commemorative book to honor an officer killed in the line of duty." Lori handed the large book, which resembled a high school annual, to her roommate. "Read it—it's not very long."

With a sigh, Sandra took the book and focused on the page. She read quietly for two or three minutes, then looked up. "Wow, this is potent. Your cop sounds like a poet."

"Doesn't he, though?" Lori giggled.

"Well, you still need to be careful. He *is* in a psychiatric ward," Sandra warned.

"He just a little depressed. There's nothing wrong with his mind. He's also one of the sexiest men I've ever met."

"Well, he *does* sound interesting. Do what you have to do. I guess he can't be much stranger than a CPA."

TEN

The ward was quiet, as it usually was on Friday evening. Apparently most people had better things to do than visit psychiatric wards on the first night of the weekend. Sage looked up from his magazine as Gordon, the hideously scarred army veteran, came through the door, looked from side to side, then eased into the chair next to his.

"Are you getting out on a pass tomorrow, Sergeant?" Gordon Platt asked from the corner of his scarred slash of a mouth, like a gangster in an old Bogart film.

Once you got used to looking at him, it wasn't so bad. It was more like looking at a plastic caricature of a monster in a low-budget movie. His hair, falling straight down his back like a horse's mane from a point halfway back on his scalp, added an element of absurdity to the face. He combed the long gray hair constantly.

"Yes, I am."

"Can you smuggle a letter out for me? It's for my father."

"Why don't you just give it to him when he comes, Gordon?"

"They'd see me."

"*Who?*" Sage put down the old *Time* magazine he had been half heartedly reading and listened with interest.

"The propaganda officer. He's responsible for the brain-washing here. I go along, pretending I don't know where I really am. I know I'm not on an American military post, though."

"Where are you then?"

"Same place you are." His eyes became sly. "In a prisoner-of-war camp somewhere near Hanoi. They won't forget us, though. One day, when the war's over, the Special Forces or Seals will come for us."

"How do you think your father gets through the lines to a prisoner-of-war camp in enemy territory?"

"I've wondered about that myself. Do you think maybe he's not really my father?"

"I don't know Gordon. I'll take the letter out and mail it for you."

"Thanks." He glanced around the room and slipped Sage a folded sheet of lined note paper. Later, David looked at it and found a manic sort of scribbling, a code that existed only in Gordon's head.

"Your father was a soldier, too, wasn't he, Gordon?"

"Certainly. It's a family tradition. All the male members of my family go off to war and win medals. I thought I wanted to be a musician once, but my father was so disappointed that I joined the army."

"When was that, Gordon?"

"Two years ago, in 1968. It was a year later when I was hit with the white phosphorous—just outside Danang. That's how I got these scars, you know, and why I was awarded the silver star for bravery. My father's very proud. To be honest, I don't think he believed I had it in me to be a soldier.

"I was always a nervous kid, afraid of my shadow. I was scared, *real* scared when I got my orders for 'Nam. I came through, though. Of course, I'm out of it now. I'd like to go back, but my burns were too bad."

"I'll see that your father gets the letter, Gordon."

David Sage watched him casually stand, then slip cautiously through the door into the hallway, trying to imagine a fear that could rob a man of thirty years of his life and make permanent disfigurement preferable to reality.

Without warning, Mr. Yow appeared in front of Sage. His hair was in wild disarray and his eyes were frantic. "Have you seen my wife?" he asked hoarsely.

"Sorry, Mr. Yow. I haven't seen her."

"Beal on deck! Beal on deck!" the old sailor yelled.

"Mr. Sage," a red-headed orderly called from the door, "there's a phone call for you."

As Sage crossed the day room, he saw Clifford Bigman sitting at a table staring like a cat at a canary across the room at Rachel, the catatonic fifteen-year-old. He had no doubt what was on his mind. The staff also knew what was on his mind. Her room was almost directly across from the nurses' station, where she could be watched constantly. Rachel stared ahead, a pleasant smile on her face. She had not again spoken to Sage or anyone else after the incident with the angry black youth, but had seemed somehow more alert—as if she was just about to come back.

"Hello," Sage said into the phone.

"Is this David Sage?"

"Yes." He was puzzled because only Jamey and his partner knew where he was.

"This is Lori."

"I'm sorry . . ."

"Lori. Lori Henderson, from Hematology."

"Sorry. I wasn't expecting you to call." It was the first time he had heard her name, though he had seen it on her nametag.

"I wanted to make sure it was still on for tomorrow?"

"Yeah. I got a pass."

"Would you like to see a movie . . . or what?"

"How about a drive up to Dove State Park for a picnic," he said on impulse. "Don't go to any trouble, though. We'll stop and pick up fried chicken or something."

"All right. I'll be there. Remember—I'm your *sister*, Lori. I don't want any problems."

"All right, Sis. I'll see you tomorrow." He hung up the phone and went to get a cup of coffee. Glancing across the room, he saw that Clifford Bigman had company and was speaking intensely to them. They were apparently his mother and father.

"Get me out of here, Mama. I can't stand bein' locked up with these crazy people!"

"I can't," she replied in a low voice. "You're going back to the hospital in Ohio as soon as there's an opening. It's nice there."

Her complexion was almost as light as Sage's, and her lips trembled as she spoke. On the other side of the table, her husband sat, mouth drawn into a tight line. His mustache was silvery, as was his hair. He had the look of an old athlete who was just beginning to go to seed.

"No, it *ain't* nice. It's just another looney bin."

"You're sick and you need help." The woman dabbed at her eyes with a handkerchief.

"*You're* the one who's sick," Clifford said, his lips pulling back over his teeth in a snarl. "You walk around half-naked, temptin' me from the time I'm little. When I try to do what comes natural, you lock me up. I'll get out. And when I do, I'll finish what I started the next time. And this old geezer beside you won't stop me!"

The woman broke into sobs. Her husband stood and helped her up, a look of total disgust on his face. He had said nothing.

"We're leaving, now, Clifford," he said, turning his back to the angry young man. "You've hurt your mother as much as you can tonight."

"Yeah, just get the hell outta here!" Clifford shouted. "You both make me sick!" An orderly moved over and stood between him and his parents as they moved away.

"I'll see you when I can," his mother said, a sob catching in her throat.

"You do that, *Mrs. Bigman.* You just do that," her son replied.

Watching Clifford and his parents depressed Sage. That, and knowing that he would be away from Gaynel for the entire weekend. He asked for a sedative and went to bed. It didn't help, though. In his dream, he walked down the dark tunnel with the eyes glowing on both sides of him. The angelic creature drew him to her with a grip of steel, pulling him toward her shredded face.

"It would be better if you'd had a millstone tied around your neck," she told him for the hundredth time.

ELEVEN

"You have a visitor out front," the orderly said.

"Thanks." Sage got up and walked to the front desk. "I'm going out on my pass," he told the nurse. "I need my medicine packet."

"Have a good time, Mr. Sage," said Nurse Grady's weekend replacement as senior nurse—one Lola McDaniel, a short, fortyish, and eternally cheerful woman. "Going to be with your family, I see."

"Right. My sister."

The orderly glanced at Sage from the corner of his eye, smiling to himself. Sage wondered briefly if he had recognized the technician from Hematology. It didn't matter, though, if he knew. Apparently he had decided not to blow the whistle on them.

"You have a *real* good time with your sister," the orderly said with a wink, unlocking the door and confirming that he knew what was going on. He was new on the ward, a tall, thin boy without prospects. Most of the orderlies in the psychiatric ward were university students studying to be something else. The young man with a ponytail and emerald stud in his left ear was a professional orderly.

"Thanks."

Lori was sitting on a small padded bench in the waiting area. She stood as Sage approached. She was wearing white shorts that were loose and roomy around the legs and a T-shirt with a teddy bear on the front. Her legs were shapely, toned, and sleek.

"Hi." She seemed a little nervous. That was not surprising, Sage decided. It was probably her first date with a psychiatric patient.

"Hi, yourself. You look very nice today." He wasn't just making small talk. She did look nice—in a college girl sort of way, the exact opposite of the dark and sultry Jamey Olivia and most other women to whom he was usually attracted.

They got on the elevator and rode down to the lobby. Neither of them spoke again until they were at the front door. He pushed it open and walked behind her.

"I've been doing some homework on you," she said.

"Oh yeah?"

"A friend of mine, Mary Sever, works for the sheriff's department as a secretary. She says you're one of the most highly decorated officers in this county. Something about a 'medal of valor' and two 'purple hearts.' I had no idea you were a hero when I threw myself at you."

"Is that what you did?" he asked.

"Well, that's how I felt. I don't know what got into me. I don't usually try to pick up strange men."

"Especially from the psychiatric ward."

"That's nothing to be ashamed of. A lot of people get depressed and need help."

"I guess you're right." He didn't ask her how many of those people had met their savior in the flesh. It didn't seem the proper time to tell her of his recent spiritual experience.

"So how did you win the medal of valor?"

"It's no big deal. With the medal and a little money I can buy a hamburger. It doesn't mean anything."

"How many people in your department have them?"

"Three. They've only been giving them out for five years. Why don't we talk about something else."

"Why does it make you uncomfortable to talk about it?" She seemed genuinely puzzled.

"Because any cop who had come along first would have done the same thing I did. An officer was down, and I went in to get him."

"Do the other two people with medals of valor feel the same way you do? Are they so modest?"

"I don't know. One of them was killed winning the medal, and the other had such severe head injuries that he's never spoken again. *That's* why it makes me uncomfortable. I never felt like I deserved it. I didn't even show up for the ceremony. I was drunk."

"Sorry." The pale, gossamer skin on the back of her neck and cheeks flushed. "I won't bring it up again."

"You don't have to be sorry. You didn't know it would make me uncomfortable."

"Where are you parked?" he asked, changing the subject.

"Around in the employees' lot."

"Would you care to stop at the front lot? I need to get something out of my car."

"Sure. You won't need anything, though. I packed a lunch and made a Thermos of tea."

"You won't have what I need. At least I don't think you will."

"Oh?" Her eyebrows arched.

"My pistol's under the seat. I never go anywhere without it."

Her thin but well-defined eyebrows arched upward. "Oh, and why is that?"

"Because the job I do induces paranoia. I seldom go anywhere that I don't run into somebody I've jailed."

"Have you ever been attacked by anyone you've put in jail—when you ran across them later, I mean?"

"No, but I was stalked once. The guy had my schedule and a picture he'd clipped from the paper in his wallet when he was killed in a car wreck. The hospital security chief called me. They also found a pocket calendar with my name and a big star on the date that was the anniversary of the day I arrested him."

"He wasn't planning a party, I guess?"

"No, I don't think so."

"Do you still want to go to Dove Lake?" she asked.

"No," he said, as if under the rush of sudden inspiration. "There's a cemetery where I'd like to have our picnic."

"A *cemetery?*"

"Yeah. I haven't been there in a long time, but I used to visit a lot when I was a kid."

"I'm game," she answered with an almost childish giggle. "I *knew* this was going to be an interesting day."

They sat on a large beach towel beside a tombstone that was inscribed: HERE LIES J. ADAMS WHO WAS MURDERED BY ALVIN KECK ON JULY 7, 1893 AD. Sage had always been fascinated by the fact that Mr. Adams, who had been murdered and was buried under the stone, had been acknowledged only by an initial while the man who allegedly murdered him had gotten his full name on the stone.

Sage had once made an effort to track down the story, but there had been no record at Claiborne County Court House of a murder that year. He decided that the stone had been so inscribed only to embarrass Alvin Keck.

"Is this your family cemetery?" Lori asked, spooning strawberries and yogurt from a plastic cup. It was her dessert. She had nibbled on a chicken leg and pasta salad while Sage had eaten the rest of the chicken, potato salad, and six deviled eggs.

"On my mother's side."

"How did you get interested in a graveyard?"

"Well, I don't come just to visit the graveyard. We'll walk over and visit the old Happy Valley Primitive Valley Church and School just as soon as you've finished eating." He lay back and lit a cigarette. There was a brief look of annoyance on her face, but she said nothing. Judging by her eating habits, she was a very health-conscious woman, but not one who made a big fuss about it.

"When do you expect to get out of the hospital?" she asked, sipping her unsweetened tea.

"I don't know. It all depends."

"On what?" She began to gather up paper plates and napkins and stuff them into a paper bag.

"Oh, on a lot of things." He toyed with the idea of telling her about Gaynel but decided against it. She did not pursue the question. Instead, she put the crumpled paper into her wicker basket and stood. Sage got up from the beach towel and she neatly folded it into a square.

"Let's get a move on," she said. "There are some ugly clouds piling up."

Sage looked at the clouds, noticing them for the first time. "If you don't like the weather in East Tennessee, then just hang around a few minutes and it will change," he said. There was a rumbling of thunder.

They put the basket into her silver Toyota and walked up a gravel path toward the crest of a hill. She carried the towel with her. Happy Valley had always been the place Sage loved most, though it was neither in a valley nor happy, for that matter. As they topped the hill, Lori took a deep breath.

"It's beautiful," she said. "It looks like a post card or a scene from a Laura Ingalls Wilder book."

"I've never thought of it that way. But you're right." The church building was white, trimmed neatly in black, large enough to seat possibly a hundred and fifty people. Beside the church was a little outdoor toilet trimmed just like the church. The school, however, a clapboard building with a door at each end, had long ago lost most of its paint. Kudzu vines had crept up and covered much of it.

"Why is the church in so much better condition than the school?" she asked.

"Well, the school hasn't been used in fifty years, not since the big elementary school was built over in Tazewell. The church was in constant use until about thirty years ago. It was built in 1792, then rebuilt in 1893 after the original building burned.

"When the land for this church was donated, it was with the condition that only the doctrine of predestination ever be preached here—that's Primitive Baptist doctrine. About the time my mother was a child, most of the members were converted by a Southern Baptist preacher and voted to leave the Primitive Baptist association. The other members sued. Before it was over, a judge ruled that neither side could use it. It's been abandoned ever since, but some of the former members come every year and paint it."

"That's a shame," she said. "It's such a beautiful old building. Can we look inside?"

"No, it's locked down by court order. We can walk over and go through the school, if you like. Vandals broke that building open years ago."

Rain began to fall, first in scattered drops, then in a deluge. They ran for the old school building but were still soaked by the time they got to the door.

His mother had attended Happy Valley School. It was a little bigger than the old one-room school houses of American mythology, but it had only two rooms. One side, his mother had once told him, had been used for first grade through fourth, the other for fifth through eighth. Several windows were out and it smelled of dust and mildew. Tattered old books, fifty years abandoned, were scattered around the room.

"I'm soaked," Lori said, pulling the teddy bear T-shirt over her head to reveal a dainty lace bra. She turned her back and unhooked the bra. The delicate ridge of her spine was barely visible through the nearly transparent skin of her back. Sage felt a stirring of heat in his groin, though he had not intended on carrying the relationship farther than a pleasant afternoon interlude. He already had too many things troubling him.

She wrapped the beach towel around her shoulders before turning to face him. The sight of her draped in a towel aroused him more than if she'd actually been naked. She must have seen something in his face.

"I'm acting like a slut, aren't I?" Her eyes did not leave his.

"We must *both* be sluts," Sage answered as he moved toward her. Her lips were on a level with his. For a moment their eyes locked, then their bodies merged in a hot embrace. They kissed intensely for a moment, before she let her lips slide around to whisper in his ear.

"I don't usually do things like this. Do you believe me?"

"Yes." He nibbled at her tiny, sculptured ear, let his tongue flicker around the inside until she shuddered violently. Her honeysuckle smell was strong in his nostrils.

"I had a bad relationship, and I haven't been with a man in over a year. But ever since the morning . . ."

"When you came in and found Jamey with her bare breasts hanging out. Is that what you mean, Lori?" Sage whispered, licking her cheek.

"Yes. *Yes*," she gasped as he slid his hands up inside the towel to cover her small breasts. The nipples were hard and cool to the touch but the skin around her breasts was smooth and warm.

"I touched myself that night while I fantasized about walking in and joining the two of you. I wanted to let you look at my bare breasts beside hers. She has big, beautiful breasts. And mine are so tiny. . . ."

She broke loose, turned and laid out the beach towel hurriedly on one end of an old, wooden table, then quickly stepped from her panties and shorts and turned to face him again, shuddering as his eyes moved over strawberry nipples and silky auburn pubic hair. "Do it now before I change my mind. Fuck me the way you fuck her!"

He walked toward her, pushing his jeans down. Reaching around, he cupped her muscular buttocks and lifted her to the table. There was only a moment of fumbling. Her legs went around his waist and she screamed in ecstasy as he entered the furnace inside her.

"Yes, yes! *Hard*, the way I know you do it to her." She reached out and pulled Sage to her, probing his mouth with her tongue.

It was short and intense. He was aware of everything and nothing, all at the same time—her honeysuckle smell, her taste, the ancient, moldy odor of old books, the rain soaking into the black loam outside.

They both exploded in spasms. With his back arched, as he attempted to probe the depth of Lori's body and soul, Sage thought of Jamey, his former savior, and of Gaynel, his savior in waiting.

In the day room of 6 North, Clifford Bigman sat staring at Rachel, the catatonic fifteen-year-old, over the top of the magazine he pretended to read. The cop was gone for the night, but it didn't help much. The girl's room was right next to the nurses' station. They would see him if he tried to go in after bedtime.

He wanted to possess her, and it was more than sexual arousal that drove him. Clifford Bigman could not verbalize his emotions, but it was a lust for power and domination that fueled his psyche, an urge to go beyond the boundaries of what the world allowed. He couldn't remember when the urge to dominate and humiliate other people had first come over him, but it continued to grow with the passing of time.

His mother was the ultimate goal of his twisted yearning. There was no power greater than that, none that he could conceive than to go back and repossess the source of his life, to push aside the man who had sired him. It was like Lucifer's dream that he would one day sit above his Creator by supplanting the throne of God. All other conquests were momentary, fleeting in nature. His mother, however, would fulfill him. Of that he was sure.

Clifford Bigman's assaults on other human beings went back farther than even his psychiatrists knew. By the age of eleven, he had already molested several smaller children. They had not told on him because they feared him. In turn, Clifford had been held in check only because he feared his father.

After the pictures of his mother had been exposed, that fear had diminished every year. His first attempt to seduce his mother had begun at the age of seventeen, when he entered her private bathroom and fondled her breasts as she sat in the tub, eyes closed, relaxed.

The reaction had not been what Clifford had fantasized. He fled the bathroom, fearing that her screams would bring one of the servants. The next day, two officers had arrived with a paper signed by a judge and Clifford Bigman had begun a long series of stays in one institution after another.

His obsession had not waned through his many periods in lock-up. Only his father's political connections had kept him out of the state hospital for the criminally insane. Clifford Bigman was an engine running without a governor, a juggernaut crushing everyone around him.

Even his parents were beginning to realize that there was no hope for him, that he could never live among civilized people. But they did not know why. How could they? Not even the psychiatrists understood it—not after seven years of complicated medical and psychiatric testing.

Clifford fondled himself surreptitiously under the table, growing an erection as he remembered the girl's bud-like nipples. He looked around the day room for a moment, then smiled to himself.

The girl was not the only accessible victim in the ward.

He got up from the table and stretched. One orderly was leaning against the counter in the hallway, talking to the second-shift nurse. The other was absorbed in a television drama. Clifford strolled into the hallway and looked up and down. The nurse and orderly ignored him.

Yawning sleepily, he walked toward his room, then turned right into the room two doors from his. It was a private room, the kind reserved for those with good insurance, one just like Clifford's. He pushed the door closed behind him as he entered.

"What do you want?" Raymond asked from the bed, obviously startled. He put down the book he had been reading. For the first time since entering the ward, Clifford saw the delicate, middle-aged law student with his hair unkempt.

"Jist thought I'd drop in for a visit," Clifford said with a toothy grin. "It's lonesome with so many people gone for the weekend. I thought we might jist talk a while."

"Well, I'm not in the mood for a visitor," Raymond said. "Please get out."

"Now don't be like that," Clifford said, advancing across the room. "We've got somethin' in common, me and you."

"What would that be?" Raymond swallowed hard and a sheen of sweat appeared on his head.

"We'll, you like to give head and I like gettin' head. *That's* what we got in common."

"Get out of here before I yell for an orderly," Raymond demanded. There was tremor in his voice, however.

"You ain't gonna do that, you old faggot. If you yell or tell *anybody*, I'll hurt you bad. Understand?"

"Please . . . ," Raymond began.

"You just be quiet and do what you're good at." Clifford laughed. It was ugly, almost theatrically diabolical laughter that came from deep in Clifford Bigman's chest as he grabbed Raymond's hair, jerked him to the floor and forced him to his knees.

TWELVE

David Sage entered the day room and drew a cup of black coffee from the urn. The breakfast cart was already at the door waiting for an orderly to hand out the trays. Lori had just dropped him off. He had slept over at her apartment Saturday night, pleased with the passionate woman who had emerged from the persona of the cool, aloof medical technician there among the moldy books and dusty tables of the old school.

In her bed he had not dreamed of tunnels, glowing eyes, and shredded flesh. But Sage had been unwilling to push too hard by asking to stay over another night. Some things are best approached slowly.

Edward was sitting at a table alone, staring into space. He had forgotten his headband that morning and his long black hair with the silver streaks fell over both shoulders loosely.

"Raymond must have overslept," Sage observed as he took a seat by the big man with the long hair.

"He isn't here," the pseudo-hippie said. "He slashed both of his wrists and his throat in the middle of the night. He got the blade out of one of those disposable razors."

"Is he going to be all right?" Sage asked, stunned.

"Yeah. He didn't get through to the carotid artery, but he

did a good job on his wrists. The night nurse found him pretty soon after it happened."

"Did something happen to upset him yesterday? That's a silly question—I mean, does anybody know *why* he was upset?"

"No. He was fine last night. Come on, let's get our trays," Edward said, rising from the table.

"I eat my eggs poached, *not scrambled.*"

Sage had never seen the woman who was standing by the food cart. The voice, however, matched that of the law professor who had been brought in kicking and screaming two days earlier and had been restrained in her room thereafter. She was a chunky woman, wearing a hospital gown, with silver-blonde hair, of perhaps fifty-five years.

"Dr. Hart," the bored orderly said, "you know perfectly well that you get what they send you until you fill out a menu. You have refused to do that."

"Don't throw your trivial, bureaucratic rules at me, you uneducated oaf. Get me two poached eggs on toast. Do it now!"

"Take the tray or go hungry," the orderly answered, color rising in his cheeks. "Makes no difference to me."

She snatched the tray from his hands, glaring at him malevolently. "I don't need a menu. I'll be out of this dump with a writ of habeas corpus before the week's over."

"Whatever you say, Dr. Hart. Now please move on so the other patients can get their trays."

"I, sir, am not a patient, but a *political prisoner.*" The law professor whirled and stalked off to a table. Her hospital gown was open at the back, revealing buttocks that looked remarkably firm for a woman her age and weight. Even more surprising was the small, neat rose tattooed on the left cheek. The staff had learned long ago, on other of her numerous visits, that she was not modest and could not be forced to conform to everyday regulations.

"She's manic depressive, bipolar," Edward said from the corner of his mouth," and she won't take her lithium."

As they took their seat, Gaynel pirouetted into the room, gracefully lifting her tray from the orderly's hands as she passed.

"I thought Gaynel was on a weekend pass?" Sage commented, looking surprised.

"That redneck she's married to brought her in last night about eleven. She was curled up in a ball, quivering all over. He made such a scene that they finally called in Dr. Wilson. They went into the conference room and talked a long time."

"About what?" Sage asked, a bite of scrambled egg on its way to his mouth.

"Who knows?" Edward replied. "One of them drives a truck and the other calls himself a psychiatrist, but they're both rednecks. They probably talked about fishing or pussy or off-the-road Jeep-driving trips."

"Get away from me, you freak. I'm tryin' to eat my breakfast. Get away *now*!"

Gordon, the melted man, was standing by Clifford Bigman's table, a look of consternation on his movie monster face. "Go on, get away from me!" The fear in Clifford Bigman's voice was genuine.

The scarred man turned and walked over to sit with Sage and Edward. "That Lieutenant Jeeter is getting meaner by the day," Gordon stated, taking a seat.

"Yeah," Edward answered, averting his eyes from Gordon's face. "He's a mean one all right."

"And he's violating military regulations," Gordon said, taking in a large mouthful of biscuits and gravy.

"What regulations?" Sage asked suspiciously.

"I can't say." Gordon chewed with his mouth open, his purplish, stretched lips looking as if they might break apart under the movement. "I don't get involved in the personal lives of officers. But if he's gonna make such a big deal out of sitting at the table with an enlisted man, he needs to study the code about personal fraternization and follow all of it, instead of just what he likes."

Sage looked at Edward, and the big man shrugged to indicate that he had no idea what Gordon was talking about.

"Did you get the letter out to my father?" Gordon asked from the corner of his mouth.

"Yeah, I got it out, Gordon," David Sage replied truthfully. He had dropped it in a mailbox, though it had no address on it.

"Good! Maybe my father will get a rescue party in this week—that is, if they haven't gotten to him, too."

"Maybe he will, Gordon."

"I'll see that this gets into your service jacket," Gordon told Sage. "It might be worth a Silver Star." The scarred man picked up his tray and left the table, having wolfed down his food in a few bites.

"Will they bring Raymond back when he's healed?" Sage asked, watching the burned army veteran walk away.

"Yeah, I think so," Edward answered, lighting a cigarette. "It's not his first attempted suicide."

Suddenly the old sailor and Mr. Yow erupted almost simultaneously.

"Beal on deck! Beal on deck!"

"*Has anybody seen my wife?*"

"Shut the fuck up!" Clifford Bigman yelled at both of them.

"This is cruel and inhuman treatment under the U.S. constitution," Dr. Hart screamed to nobody in particular.

"This is going to be a *long* Sunday," Sage sighed.

"You're right," Edward answered, as Gaynel danced by their table, humming "Amazing Grace."

"Daddy, when's Mama comin' home to stay?" the eight-year-old boy asked, picking at the burnt scrambled eggs with distaste.

"Real soon, I hope," George Potts replied to his son, not looking directly at the boy, who secretly disgusted him because he was puny and had inherited Gaynel's bad vision. He was the kind of little boy that George Potts had called "four-eyes" and "sissy" when he was a school athlete. Sometimes, when he was drinking, he would call his son those names.

"What got her upset last night?" the little boy asked.

"I just asked her to be a wife to me, that's all," the big man said, gulping a cup of scalding black coffee. "That's all."

"What's that mean?" the boy asked. "She was all right when she went to bed."

"You wouldn't understand," George Potts said, glancing at his daughter, who was glaring at him. She was fourteen and understood *perfectly*. Her room was right next to her parents'.

"What're you glarin' at?" George Potts snapped.

"Nothin'." She stared at her plate. "Why do you think Mom's comin' home soon?" The girl had become uneasy lately. She didn't like the way her father was looking at her.

"I talked to her new psychiatrist last night," Potts told his daughter. "The pussyfootin' around is gonna stop. I've fired that pencil-necked wimp Wohlford. Dr. Wilson is going to give your mama the kind of treatment she needs to get better."

"What's that?" his daughter asked suspiciously.

He burped loudly before answering. "It's called 'lectro-convulsive therapy. They run 'lectricity through a crazy person's head to make 'em sane again."

"How's that supposed to help?"

"I don't know," George Potts answered, slurping his coffee. "Maybe it just makes 'em so damned uncomfortable that they don't want to lay on their lazy butts in a hospital anymore. It can't make things any worse, can it?"

"I don't know," the girl replied with a shudder. "When is this going to happen?"

"*Real* soon," George Potts answered smugly. "Real soon."

"You awake, Dave?" Edward asked across the dark room.

"Yes I am, Edward."

"You were right. This is one of the longest Sundays I can remember. Gaynel preaching to Dr. Hart was the high point of the day."

"Yeah," Sage answered. Gaynel's attempt to bless the law professor had resulted in an hour of lectures on atheistic secular humanism from the professor.

"I think I'm an atheist, like Dr. Hart," Edward said.

"That's certainly your privilege, Edward."

"I was raised a Methodist, but I never really took it seriously. Were you raised in church?"

"Yes, Edward. I was raised a Baptist. Fortunately, I escaped without permanent damage, I think."

"Then how come you believe that the savior talks directly to you? Baptists don't believe that sort of thing, do they?"

"Sure they do. Baptists talk to God all the time. They talk

more than they listen. As a matter of fact, most religious people talk to God more than they listen."

"Not in person," Edward said. "They don't talk to the savior in the flesh. That's what I meant."

"I don't know about other people," David Sage said.

"Do you think Gaynel believes that she really is the savior?"

"Yeah, I think she believes that she's really the savior. Why do you ask, Edward?"

"Because I think you believe Gaynel's the savior, too."

"Oh? . . ."

"You watch her all the time," Edward finally said. "Even when you're doing other things, you watch her like you're expecting something to happen just anytime."

The room grew quiet.

"I guess you don't want to discuss Gaynel," Edward said.

"Not really."

"Do you believe in miracles, David?"

"How do you define a miracle, Edward?"

"Supernatural intervention. Something that couldn't have happened by itself."

"You mean like the seagulls at Salt Lake City?"

"What are you talking about?"

"I'm told that the Mormons were about to lose their first crop to locusts in their early days in Utah," Sage answered, "and seagulls swooped down out of the sky and ate the locusts."

"Did that really happen? Seagulls in the middle of Utah?" Edward asked suspiciously.

"So I hear."

"Somebody could have made up that story. Has anything like that ever happened to you personally?"

"When I was in the first grade, there was something that *seemed* like a miracle."

"Tell me about it."

"We made our first trip to the library," Sage began, "and I was overwhelmed by the number of books in that school library. They only let us have one book each and they told us that if we lost it we'd never be able to get another one. . . ."

"And you lost it, right?"

"Do you want me to tell this story, Edward?"

"Sorry. Go ahead."

"I checked out a little book called *Noah's Ark*. I still remember exactly what it looked like. It was gray with red lettering and had a line drawing of an elephant walking up the ramp onto the ark. I was so excited about that book that I was shaking all the way back to the classroom.

"It was real cold that day, so I tucked it under my arm as tightly as I could. At one of the cross streets, a safety patrol boy—they didn't have women in law enforcement then—asked me if he could look at it. He was only about twelve, but to a first grader, a twelve-year-old, and a safety patrol boy at that, is like God.

"He was a nice person, not one of those kids who let power go to their heads. He congratulated me on my taste in books, and I went on my way.

"Only, when I got home, the book wasn't under my arm anymore. It had slipped out. I was terrified. We were allowed to keep the books for two weeks at a time and I lived in terror for those two weeks."

"Did you tell anyone?" Edward asked.

"No. Not even my mom. I left for school the morning that book was due, sick with worry. Then, just as we got to the crossing where the patrol boy had stopped me two weeks earlier, I noticed that the little boy walking ahead of me had my *Noah's Ark* under his arm. He lived two houses from me. I demanded the book, but he said he had found it on the sidewalk and his mother had told him to return it to the library.

"I was almost in tears and screaming for my book, when that same patrol boy who had looked at the book two weeks earlier came up to see what the excitement was about.

"When I told him that the other kid had my book, he looked at it and told the other kid that it belonged to me. I got to school with my book and nobody was ever the wiser. I always considered that a miracle."

"*That's it?*" Edward sounded surprised.

"I'm afraid so."

"I'm not even a cop and I could come up with a better story than that. That wasn't a *miracle*, it was just a *coincidence*."

"Maybe that's all *any* miracle is," Sage replied.

THIRTEEN

The dream tunnel seemed damper, hotter, and darker than usual, and the terror was an oppressive blanket that smothered David Sage as he walked down the dark passage, red eyes glowing on each side of him, their mystery owners waiting for him to stray too far from the center.

He approached the wooden door, swallowing hard. Opening it with a growing sense of dread, he saw the beautiful female creature with the peaches and cream complexion and the pink nipple, standing with her right side to him. She grabbed him by the wrist with a grip of steel and pulled him toward her.

"You would have been better off with a millstone . . ."

"David. *David!* Wake up."

His eyes opened widely, a look of terror in them. Lori stood over him, concern showing in her own green eyes.

"You're soaked with sweat. What's wrong?" she asked, wiping his forehead with a gauze pad. "Bad dream?"

He swallowed hard, bringing his shudders under control. "Yeah, but you woke me up just as the worst part was about to happen."

"Care to tell me about it?" She laid her cool hand on his

cheek, and her honeysuckle and isopropyl alcohol smell teased his nostrils.

"Some day, but not this morning," he answered.

"When?"

"When I'm save . . . when I'm cured."

"Are you expecting to be cured soon?" She looked around, then leaned forward and kissed him lightly on the lips with lingering tenderness.

"Well, does *every* patient get this kind of treatment at Municipal Hospital?"

Lori whirled around and saw Jamey, standing akimbo at the door. She was dressed in a simple black suit and had her hair up. The change in style made her look more like a businesswoman than the lusty vixen Lori had first seen standing bare-breasted by David's bed. Lori's cheeks colored and she fumbled through her basket, as if unable to recognize the tools of her trade.

"I leave you alone for a few days, Lovah, and you betray me with a redhead. What am I going to do with you?"

"I'm . . . I'll be back later." Lori quickly left the room, eyes on the floor.

"Lori, wait!" David called to her, but she didn't look back.

"Well?" Jamey asked.

"Well, *what*?"

"Have you betrayed me with that redhead? Have you slept with her?" David was not sure whether her anger was real or merely a show.

"It's impossible for me to betray you, Jamey, because you've never offered me anything permanent."

"Only because I *can't*, Lovah." She moved close to him. "In a month we'd destroy each other if we lived together."

"I know," Sage said tiredly.

"You *have* slept with that girl, though." Jamey took a pack of long, thin cigarettes from her purse and lit two.

"How do you know that?"

"Because"—she blew a stream of smoke, then put one of the cigarettes in Sage's mouth—"she was kissing you, just then, the way a woman kisses her lover."

"How do you know she wasn't just trying to seduce me?"

"I just *know*. I'm a woman and what I just saw was a *done deed*. That child is in love with you."

"I doubt that," Sage replied, rising to his elbow and drawing deeply on the cigarette. "She doesn't know me that well."

"You're not hard to love, David. You think you're a grizzly bear, but you're really just a cuddly little teddy bear. I fell in love with you *before* I seduced you. I was already in love with your pain. You were such a sick little boy—but you're getting better. I can see that."

"Oh yeah?"

"So, did it happen here or did you go out over the weekend?"

"That's a pretty personal question."

"You're right." Jamey stubbed out the cigarette in an ashtray on the bedside table. "I just wanted to check in on you. I need to be going so your kitten can come back and do her job."

"You're not upset, are you?"

"No." She leaned over and kissed him lightly on the mouth. "Just a little sad that I'm losing you."

"You'll *never* lose me, Jamey."

"Oh yes I will. You're too much of a bluenose to sleep with two women at the same time. I'll see you later."

She was out the door before he could reply, and a few minutes later a technician he had never seen came to draw his blood.

After the phlebotomist had finished drawing his blood, Sage dressed and went to the day room for breakfast. Edward was already in his seat by the window, staring out. His days in the ward were dwindling away, and he was depressed.

Katrina stood by one of the tables playing a frenetic game of solitaire, bouncing from one foot to the other. The electro-convulsive therapy had less effect on her every time they used it. Mr. Beal, on the other hand, was slumped forward in the wheelchair, saliva dripping from his mouth, eyes closed, where the orderlies had left him a few minutes earlier. Within a half-hour, he would awaken, a dazed expression in his eyes. It would be afternoon before he began yelling again.

At the back of the day room, Gaynel moved in a slow, solitary waltz, a look of bliss on her homely face. Sometimes Sage wondered what she was thinking but never asked. All things would be revealed in good time.

Clifford Bigman came to the door and looked before entering to make certain the man with the scarred face was not waiting to talk to Lieutenant Jeeter. No amount of screaming on Clifford's part would dissuade the man from his fixation.

The catatonic Rachel sat smiling angelically by the wall. She looked slowly around, but said nothing to Mr. Yow who sat beside her, having a quiet time for a change.

"I heard the night nurse tell Grady that Raymond is doing better this morning. He may be back in tomorrow," Edward said as Sage approached the table, sipping coffee and lighting a cigarette.

"That's good. I just wonder what happened." He took a deep drag on the cigarette.

"Who knows?" Edward shrugged. "Raymond's not very stable."

"You mean, he's not as stable as the rest of us?" Sage asked.

"You know what I mean. He's *delicate*. Something made you break, but basically, you're tough."

"I'm glad *you* know so much about me," Sage retorted, remembering that he *had* once believed in himself, in his ability to do anything he chose and to make decisions under pressure.

On the rare occasions when he had appeared in Internal Affairs *before* the Lyda Herrel case, Sage had always been like a man of iron. Nobody at the department had ever seen him sweat—especially the shooflies. He had always made his decisions and stood by them.

The last time, though, things had been different. . . .

"All right," Clint Beamer said, running his finger around the inside of his pastel pink collar as if choking, "let's go over this again." The Internal Affairs Division had once been a rotating job for the most part, because of the lonely nature of the work. Most cops had trouble dealing with the loss of camaraderie. Sergeant Clint Beamer, however, had little to lose. He had been held in contempt by most Knox County officers even before *volunteering* for the Internal Affairs job.

As a sergeant on Charlie Shift, as detachments have always been called at the department, Beamer's official call sign had been "Charlie four," denoting that he was fourth in command. His main contribution to the shift had always been to insist that everyone wear a hat, even at night when nobody was watching except drunk drivers and thieves. His own hat, worn pulled snugly down, left a bright red ring around his bald pate when he took it off. Behind his back, the other officers called him "*Circumcision* four."

"The patrol officer called you just before three in the

morning. What was it he told you?" Beamer asked.

"That he had a case he didn't know how to classify," Sage told him for the fifth time.

"And what kind of classification did you give it?"

"You've got it in front of you!"

"Answer the question," the chubby sergeant said.

"I classified it as an 'incident/miscellaneous.'"

"Why that?"

"Because there was no other classification for it!"

"What about 'missing person/infant'?" Beamer asked.

"Because I had no way to prove that an infant had ever existed," Sage replied tiredly.

"The doctor said—"

The Internal Affairs investigator looked at his notes.

"And Oral Roberts once said that he saw a five-hundred-foot Jesus. I wouldn't have risked my career on *his* word, either."

"After the doctor told you that Lyda Herrel had delivered a full-term baby, what did you do?"

Sage lit a cigarette and inhaled deeply. "I went to the residence Lyda Herrel had given as an address. Once there, I interviewed her parents, who claimed that they had no knowledge that their daughter was pregnant. I asked to search the house, but they refused permission."

"Her parents say you didn't ask permission to search," Beamer countered, once more running his finger around the inside of his collar.

"They're lying," Sage said with a shrug.

"Why would they lie?"

"Oh, come on, Beamer. If you'd caused the death of a baby by refusing to cooperate, would you admit it? Besides, they probably think the county will pay them bucks if they threaten a nuisance suit."

"With the possibility that a newborn infant was somewhere in the house without anyone to look after it, why didn't you go ahead and search anyway?"

"That's crap! If I'd done it and there *hadn't* been a baby, you'd have had me in here asking me why I violated their civil rights by searching without a warrant or probable cause."

"Did you try to obtain a search warrant?"

"No, I *didn't*. If I'd had *probable cause*, I would have searched without a warrant."

"Why?" Sergeant Beamer asked.

"Because of exigent circumstances. It was a case where—if I'd *had* probable cause—waiting for a warrant would have risked the baby's life."

"So why *didn't* you search?" Beamer pressed.

Sage's head went to his chest and tears began to roll down his face. A surge of triumph shot through the IAD officer's chest. He had made the Ironman cry.

"It's time for group," the blond orderly with a ponytail and earring said. "Did you hear me, Mr. Sage? Are you all right?"

"Oh, sorry, I had my mind somewhere else," Sage answered, coming back from the memory of the Internal Affairs interview. He realized he had real tears in his eyes. "I'm fine, thanks."

He quickly brushed his eyes with the back of his hand and followed the orderly to the group therapy room and took his place in the circle, noting that he was the last to arrive.

"Who wants to begin this morning?" Nurse Grady asked.

Down the hall, Dr. Hart was screaming and cursing. Her screams were muffled, but they could still be heard all over the ward. The law professor had refused to attend group therapy, and Nurse Grady had ordered her to be escorted by an orderly to the therapy room. Before it was over, Dr. Hart was once again restrained to her bed where she spent most of her time anyway.

"Does anyone know what upset Raymond Saturday night?" Sage inquired.

"I guess we'll just have to wait and ask him when he gets back," Nurse Grady replied primly. "We don't discuss patients when they're not here."

"He was fine when he told me goodnight," Katrina said, shifting on her folding chair. "I can't imagine what happened."

"Maybe he heard some bad news from home or something," Edward said.

"Naw, he would have told someone," Katrina replied.

"Please!" Nurse Grady said. "Didn't you hear what I just said? *We don't discuss patients when they aren't here.* Now, does anyone want to work on his or her problems today?"

"I do," Edward said.

"Go ahead."

"Mr. Beal is missing the toilet bowl and peeing on the floor again. Can't we restrict him to the handicapped restroom? Nobody else uses it."

"Edward, Mr. Beal's personal habits are not what I had in mind when I asked if anyone wanted to work on a personal problem," the nurse said.

"Well, it's important to me," Edward said sulkily. If Mr. Beal heard Edward's comment, he didn't respond.

"Gaynel, you haven't talked in a while," the nurse noted, choosing to ignore Edward.

Gaynel, who had been sitting quietly across the circle from David Sage, opened her eyes briefly, smiled, then closed them again without answering.

"I have a question," Mr. Yow said, unfolding his arms and looking at the members of the group.

"We welcome your comments," Nurse Grady said, nodding perkily.

"Has anyone seen my wife?" Then again, louder, "*Has anyone seen my wife?*"

Everyone sat quietly as the orderly led Mr. Yow away, sobbing and screaming at the top of his lungs.

"Clifford, do you have anything to say?" the nurse inquired.

"Nah, I got nothin' to say except actions speak louder than words. I've always believed that, always will. People can try to hide what they are, but it always comes out eventually." He was sitting next to Katrina, arms crossed, legs stretched in front of him, a sneer on his face.

"Would you care to elaborate on that?"

"Nah." Clifford Bigman's yellow eyes were fixed on David Sage. Briefly, Sage wondered what Bigman was trying to convey. But only for a moment. He had faced people like Clifford Bigman hundreds of times during interrogations. Even when they did not speak, their sly glances and the smugness of their eyes told the story—a silent boast about what they had gotten away with.

The detective suddenly knew with total certainty that Clifford had been responsible for Raymond's suicide attempt. The realization left him chilled. When the big man's eyes met Sage's and he saw that Sage had figured it out, he smiled smugly and looked away.

David Sage barely kept himself from crossing the circle of chairs and beating Clifford Bigman. The detective had only seen such malignant hatred once before in his career and it had been in the eyes of a woman named Lyda Herrel. He trembled with rage as he sat through the rest of the therapy session.

∞

"Did you have a pleasant weekend?" Dr. Chavez Wilson asked, his pen poised to make notations on Sage's chart.

"It was all right."

"Did your hallucination about the savior recur outside the ward?"

"No, but I had a visitation as soon as I got back. It was just as plain as ever."

"No change, then. I'm going to leave everything as is right now. If things continue as they are, we'll discuss a different therapy in a few days."

David Sage nodded noncommittally as the psychiatrist made a brief note and moved on to Edward's table. *It's all claptrap anyway,* Sage thought, *mindless pyschobabble, about two steps removed from the snakepits. And you're nothing but a witch doctor with a Ph.D.*

"What kind of weekend did you have, Edward, aside from the demons?" the doctor inquired.

"The voices are telling me to kill myself. Not that it matters to you," Edward said sullenly.

"Don't ruin what's been a lovely relationship by being sullen, Edward," Dr. Wilson said. "You've already been here longer than policy allows."

"Yes, but . . ."

Having made a brief notation, Dr. Chavez Wilson had already moved to the couch where Gaynel was sitting with her eyes closed.

"Gaynel, open your eyes."

"Yes, my child."

"Things can't go on this way. You have to start taking part in your own healing."

"I have no need of healing," Gaynel replied with a smile. "I am here to heal."

"Have it your way, Gaynel. But I've talked to your husband, and if we don't get some cooperation from you, we're going to consider a more aggressive therapy."

"Whatever you say, my child." He made a note on her chart and moved on.

Sage had listened closely to the exchange. He didn't like the sound of *more aggressive therapy*. He was glad that Dr. Wohlford was Gaynel's *real* doctor. No telling what Dr. Wilson might try. Sage wondered if there was a snake pit hidden away somewhere for the ducktailed psychiatrist's use.

As Dr. Wilson was making his rounds on 6 North, Lyda Herrel was getting back the items taken from her on her arrival at the Horton County Jail the previous evening. She sat, dwarfing her chair, as the young female officer laid each item on the table, checking each off in turn. It felt good to be in nice civilian clothes again after two years. Lyda's mother had sent her a beautiful dress to wear home from jail. It was yellow and white gingham, made with enough material to construct a small circus tent.

"One brush, one lipstick, one watch, gold in color, one toothbrush and tube of toothpaste—Colgate. Sign here to show that you got everything back that you came in with," said the officer, who was clad in blue poplin.

"Everything but the two years of my life that David Sage stole from me," Lyda answered, taking the ballpoint pen in her sausage-like fingers and scrawling an illegible signature at the bottom of the page. Lyda hated skinny women, skinny women being those under two hundred pounds.

The young officer's lip curled in contempt. She swallowed the words she wanted to say because she knew it would be pointless. Everyone in the jail, officers and prisoners alike, knew what Lyda had done. That was why she had been kept in administrative segregation all night awaiting the arrival of her release papers.

"If you'll follow me," the jailer said, "I'll take you to the front door."

"It's about time. My granny's slow, but she's old."

Is your granny a pig, too? the blonde jailer thought, but did not say. She knew Lyda's mother was a pig because everyone had been talking about her since her arrival in the jail lobby. The senior Herrel woman couldn't sit down because the chairs in the lobby were too small for her butt.

"Open up for Ms. Lyda Herrel," the blonde jail officer yelled ahead, walking deliberately fast so that Lyda had to almost run to keep up. She followed, huffing and puffing. The male, crewcut jailer inserted the large brass key and opened a door to the sally port.

"As you say, corrections officer Shelby Whaley. Your wish is my command." He bowed at the waist as the officer took Lyda into the sally port, then locked the door behind them. They stood in the small room as an officer outside the port opened the door from his side. Both doors were never opened at the same time.

Lyda Herrel pushed by Officer Whaley, almost crushing the thin blonde woman in the door. Her parents were waiting, her mother in a dress covered with red flowers and her father in his usual bibbed overalls.

"My baby!" Lyda's mother lumbered across the lobby, arms extended.

"Cut the crap, Mama," Lyda said, pushing past her. "You two go get the truck and meet me at the front door. I got somebody to see before I leave here."

"But Lyda, honey, you just got home—" her mother began.

"*Just do what I said!* I'll be outside when I get through. Just make sure you're in front of the building."

Detective Larry Ware sat in his cubicle staring glumly at his desk. A week's worth of odds and ends and scribbled phone numbers were scattered across the surface or tacked to the flimsy cubicle walls.

He paused for a moment and listened as the main door to the detective division opened. He heard a brief exchange between the morning receptionist and another woman. It was too early for most detectives to have interviews scheduled.

Ware turned to look down the aisle and saw a behemoth of a woman coming toward him. Her handmade yellow and white gingham dress made her appear even bigger than she really was. Her neck was buried in rolls of fat and the flesh of her upper arms hung past her elbows.

Jesus! Larry thought. *It's Lyda Herrel!*

She stopped at the cubicle and stared down at him from eyes sunk in pockets of fat, yet still managing to glow with some sort of hidden rage. "Do you like my new dress, Larry?"

"What?" Ware was caught off guard.

"I *said*, 'Do you like my new dress?'"

"No. It makes you look like you weigh an extra ton."

"I like a sense of humor in a black man," she said. "Along with other things."

"What do you want?" Ware growled, as if speaking to a puddle of scum on the floor.

"I wanted to see Detective David Sage, but the skinny little secretary said he's on sick leave."

"He is," Ware replied, "but if I were you, I'd stay away from him."

"Is that supposed to scare me?"

"Take it however you want. That's my advice. What do you want anyway? Maybe I can help."

"You can help with *one* of my problems. I'm horny and I've been locked up two years. Can you help me out with that? My last lover was black, you know." She put her hand on her gargantuan hip and thrust it to the side in a parody of coquettishness.

"Your last lover was obviously not a self-respecting black man," Ware retorted. "What *do* you want with Detective Sage?"

"Just wanted to let him know I'm out. He did his best to steal my life, but I'm free! When my parents get through with their lawsuit against the county for wrongful death, I'll be *rich,* too."

"Don't have a shred of regret do you?" Ware asked, looking her full in the face.

"Why should I? I was *sick* you know. 'Postpartum depression,' the psychiatrist said."

"You're not sick. You're evil. Now, if you don't need anything official, I have work to do."

"I'd like a copy of the first report Detective Sage filled out on me," she demanded.

"That would be an offense report. Records will make you one for five dollars. Good-bye."

"I don't have any money. They just let me out and my parents are on their way to get me. It won't look good when

I get to court if I tell my lawyer you wouldn't cooperate with me."

There was a hot reply on Ware's lips, but he bit it back. Instead, he got his keys out, opened Sage's locked filing cabinet and found what Lyda Herrel wanted. He stepped around the corner and made a copy and was back in less than a minute.

"Here it is. Good day."

"Thank you ever so much, Detective Ware." She turned, a look of triumph on her face, and waddled away.

"Evil bitch!" Ware muttered to himself. He went back to straightening up his desk and never noticed that the small note with David Sage's hospital room number had vanished. There were too many other little notes for one to be missed.

FOURTEEN

"We're glad to see you back, Raymond," the night nurse said.

The aging law student, with bandages on both wrists and on one side of his throat, only nodded as the orderly signed his transfer papers and remanded him back to the care of the psychiatric wing an hour before breakfast.

He didn't know why they had brought him so early in the morning, but he was glad that it hadn't been necessary for him to walk into the crowded day room. If he was there when everyone came in, it wouldn't feel so much like they could tell what had happened to him just by looking.

"Thank you," Raymond replied. His wispy hair was uncombed, and he was wearing a robe over wrinkled pajamas. He went into the day room and drew himself a steaming cup of fresh coffee. The melted man was sitting silently on the other side of the room.

As Raymond took his seat, Gaynel swirled through the door on her toes, a beatific smile on her face, and gracefully took the coffee from his hand. He watched her pirouette away, then went to get another cup.

"I'm glad to see you back," David Sage said as he came through the day room door and walked over to the coffeepot.

"Thanks," Raymond answered listlessly, taking a seat at a nearby table.

"Can we talk?" Sage asked, pulling out a chair.

"Maybe," Raymond answered. "Do you have an extra cigarette? Mine are in my room and I haven't been there yet. My hair must look a fright."

"You look fine for a man who tried to kill himself over the weekend."

"Are you going to ask why?"

"I think I know why, generally speaking," Sage answered, lighting two cigarettes and handing one to Raymond.

"That obvious, huh? Is 'cocksucker' written across my head in red letters?"

"No. I'm a cop, remember? None of the staff suspect it, and as far as I know, none of the patients do, either."

"Who cares about an old queer anyway?" Raymond asked.

"I care." Sage took a drag of his cigarette, then a sip of coffee.

"Well, I think Clifford Bigman is right. You couldn't get a *normal* man to go down on you. I must have been born a queer."

"How you get off doesn't matter, Raymond. Every human being has the right to say no to unwanted advances."

"He was too strong to fight, and he said he'd hurt me if I told anyone."

"That's past. You didn't yell for help then, but you can *still* fight back."

"How?" the law student asked, holding his Styrofoam cup with a trembling hand.

"Take out a warrant charging him with aggravated rape so that he doesn't get away with it again."

"Surely you're joking? You want me to admit that I orally copulated another man, just because he *told* me to?"

154

"No, because he *coerced* you. That's aggravated rape. Nobody should get away with that."

"I'm sorry to disappoint you, David, but I don't have the kind of courage it takes to stand up and speak out. But this has cleared up a lot of things for me. I *know* what I have to do now."

"Raymond, if you're still suicidal—"

"I'm *not*," Raymond interrupted, getting up. "And just this once I don't need any help at all." The slender man walked away, back straight and chest out. Sage started to say something else, but was interrupted.

"Sergeant Sage, you're up early this morning."

He turned and smiled as Lori put her basket on the card table. "And you are looking lovely today, Lori. Why did you send a stranger to take my blood yesterday morning?"

"Because, when I saw your friend Jamey, I was suddenly embarrassed. I felt as if she would know everything that happened by just looking at me."

"Yeah, she pretty much did," Sage told her as she tightened the rubber band around his arm and tapped for a vein.

"Was she angry?"

"No, just a little sad."

"Why?" Lori asked, filling the tube with blood and quickly replacing it with another.

"She says I'm too much of a bluenose to sleep with two women at the same time," Sage replied.

"Is that true?"

"Yeah, probably so. Though I guess it *is* a little warped when you consider that I've been committing adultery with Jamey for several months."

"I wouldn't say that." She put a pad on the injection site. "She sounds like an intelligent woman. And she does have good taste in men." Lori's pale skin flushed.

"She also says you're in love with me."

"That may be just a little premature, Detective Sage. I never fall in love until at least the second date. Which reminds me, are you going out on pass this weekend?"

"Don't you have any normal friends?" he teased.

"None that are as interesting as you."

"Well then, let's make a tentative date," he said. "If I'm still a patient here this weekend—or even if I'm not."

"Do you expect to get out soon?"

"I really don't know. I'm just waiting to see what happens on a daily basis." Even as he was speaking, Gaynel danced by, eyes closed as if in ecstasy, humming "I'll Fly Away."

"They tell me you're a practitioner of law enforcement." Dr. Hart sat down at the table with David Sage, fishing out a filtered Camel cigarette. Surprisingly, her hair seemed to have had a comb run through it, and she was actually in a bathrobe.

"Yeah," Sage replied. "And they tell me you're a lawyer."

"No, no, no! A lawyer *practices* law. I just teach it. One class after another of bright-eyed young wannabes. Why would anyone want to be a lawyer, Officer Sage?"

"Damned if I know," Sage replied. "To make cops miserable, I guess."

"Not bad," she said. "Do you know why there's never been a shark attack on a lawyer?"

"Professional courtesy, I'd imagine." Sage took out an unfiltered Lucky Strike and lit it.

"Very good. If a bus filled with lawyers drove over the Grand Canyon and there was an empty seat, what would you call it?"

"A crying shame," Sage shot back.

"Do you know any others?" she asked.

"How does a puppy differ from a lawyer?" Sage asked her.

"Tell me," she replied, putting both elbows on the table.

"Given the opportunity, very few people would stomp a puppy to death. Also, the puppy will eventually grow up and stop whining."

"What are you in for?" Dr. Hart asked.

"Depression," Sage answered.

"You have *half* of my disease," she said smugly. "I'm bipolar. That's what they used to call manic-depressive."

"I'm familiar with the term," he said. "Can't they stabilize you with medicine?"

"Sure they can. I just don't take it."

"That seems a little self-destructive."

"You remember what it used to feel like on Christmas morning, Officer? Or what it felt like the first time you saw a naked woman?"

"Yeah, I remember both experiences."

"Well, *that's* the way I feel all the time when I'm manic. It's like having a month-long fucking orgasm," the law professor told him.

"Yeah, but eventually you get so far out that they have to tie you to the bed."

"Well, life's always a tradeoff," she said, putting out one cigarette, then lighting another. "Did you know I'm barred by court order from every office at the University of Tennessee right now?" She sounded proud.

"I didn't know it. You sound all right now. Are you about to get stabilized?" Sage asked, taking a sip of cranberry juice left over from breakfast.

"Yeah, unfortunately I am. Don't be surprised if I'm gone

tomorrow morning. I have one of my students filing a writ of habeas corpus today."

"Well, good luck," Sage said, assuming that the law professor was probably delusional.

"I don't need luck, I know the law," she replied.

It was the last time Sage talked to her. She was gone before breakfast the next morning.

The patients sat in a circle for the morning group therapy. The old sailor Mr. Beal and Katrina were gone for ECT, but everyone else slouched in their chairs, except for Raymond who was sitting bolt upright.

"Well," Nurse Grady began, "everyone looks chipper this morning." She was wearing a new shade of lipstick and it appeared that she had applied it in the dark or without a mirror. The hot red color made her teeth look even larger than usual. "Why don't you share this morning, Gaynel."

"I always share, my child. This body is a living sacrifice." Gaynel's head was back and her eyes were closed. "Whosoever will may come unto me."

Sage was immediately alert. *Was the moment at hand?*

"Very well, Gaynel," Nurse Grady said with a sigh. "Raymond, would you like to share with us this morning?"

"Yes, as a matter of fact I would. I'd like to talk about cruel, vicious people and why they get away with the things they do." He cast a look at Clifford Bigman who was sitting, arms crossed and legs stretched out in front of him. Bigman snorted contemptuously and returned the gaze.

"Well, go ahead, Raymond," Nurse Grady said.

"Cruel people get away with the things they do because

victims let them," the aging law student said.

"That's not necessarily so—" Sage began.

"David, *please!*" Raymond snapped. "I'm now prepared to take responsibility for my life for the first time! *Let me do it!*"

"Sorry," Sage said quietly.

"Yeah, let the little sissy talk. It outta be a hoot if he's gonna tell us about how to be brave." Clifford Bigman smirked.

Raymond shot an angry glance at Bigman, then went on. "Victims can't help being physically weaker, but they can teach a lesson to all the bullies of the world when they get tired of being abused. *I'm* not only tired of being a victim, but I'm ready to put an end to it. *Today.*"

"Whatcha gonna do, Raymond? Threaten to bite off somebody's dick the next time they make you get down on your knees?" Clifford Bigman asked with a sneer.

"No, Clifford. I'm not going to be on my knees. Not ever again!" The thin and pale fortyish law student's face was flushed.

"Well, *I'm* nervous," Bigman said, not realizing what he had just alluded to. Nurse Grady picked up on it, however, and quickly looked at Raymond.

"You *should* be nervous, Clifford. You are my bridge at Concord—you know, where the shot that was heard around the world was fired."

Clifford Bigman rolled his eyes. "Now I got no idea what you're talkin' about, sissy-boy," Clifford sneered.

"Let me make it simple then." Raymond rose without warning. "I want you to go down on this!" The thin man's arm arced upward as he stood and stepped across the circle toward Clifford Bigman, whose eyes flared open in fear. He raised his arms to protect himself.

Sage might have missed it had he not already been on alert—put there by reading Raymond's body language, a skill that the police officer had honed during hundreds of hours on the street. As it was, he barely moved in time to grab Raymond's arm and stop the shiny pointed blade from penetrating Clifford's right eye. For a moment it hovered there as Raymond pushed against Sage's grip, trying to drive the blade into Bigman's eye.

"*Abuse somebody else you brainless animal!*" Raymond screamed. "*And watch for me the rest of your life. I'll hunt you down and kill you someday!*"

As Sage wrested what he saw was a letter opener, a replica of a double-edged dagger, from Raymond's grasp, Clifford Bigman turned his chair over in an effort to get away and crashed to the floor, scrambling backward.

"Get that crazy queer outta here!" Bigman screamed. "He tried to kill me. My father will send him to the penitentiary!"

"I've got him, Mr. Sage. Turn loose," said the orderly who had been standing by.

Sage released the law student, and the orderly propelled him toward the door, holding both of his arms behind him. "Remember *Big*-man," Raymond yelled over his shoulder. "I'll be looking for *you!*"

"Put him in restraints," Nurse Grady ordered.

"I have not brought peace, but a sword," Gaynel murmured just before she pirouetted out of the room.

FIFTEEN

Lyda Herrel steered her father's old Ford pickup truck onto the interstate. When her parents were gone, she intended to sell the farm to be subdivided and make lots of money. There'd be no more old rattling pickup trucks for her. She would buy a Corvette and move to a condo in town. "Go to hell!" she screamed at the angry driver of a white van she had almost sideswiped with the sluggish old truck, as he blew his horn.

It felt good to be on the road again, to go anywhere she wanted. For two years she had been confined to a cell and the exercise yard once a day. They had kept Lyda segregated at the prison, for her own good they said because the other inmates wanted to hurt her. She had Detective David Sage to thank for that.

Now David Sage was confined in his own little prison. When she had called and asked about him, the switchboard had refused to confirm or deny that he was at Municipal Hospital. But he was there all right, locked up in the padded ward. Lyda had his hospital address, which his jungle bunny partner had been nice enough to leave on the desk. She had already known that Sage was a weakling. Not tough enough to be a cop. Cops didn't cry the way she had seen David Sage cry when he arrested her for murder.

Two years she had sat in a cell because of Sage. If he had arrived a few minutes later that day, none of the things that had happened to Lyda would have appeared. And for what? A mewling little half-breed that probably would have died anyway.

It was payback time, however, and today Lyda was going to make the first payment. *Wouldn't little David be surprised to see her walking around as a free woman?* And her lawyer had assured her that there would not be another trial.

She wheeled into the parking lot of Municipal Hospital with a smile on her face.

"Raymond really meant to kill Clifford, didn't he?" Edward asked Sage, tossing his long black hair with the silver streaks back out of his face. He was not wearing his headband.

"He was graveyard serious," Sage replied, taking a bite of what was euphemistically called a "meat roll" but was actually biscuit dough with a thin coating of meat sauce spread inside. The other choice for the day had been baked chicken, which generally came unseasoned, and was served either burned to a crisp or half raw. Gaynel glided gracefully around the day room, taking nibbles from her own meat roll.

"What was it he tried to kill Clifford with?" Edward inquired.

"It was a letter opener. He probably bought it down in the gift shop while he was off lock-up being treated for his cuts."

"You think this change will last? Or will Raymond go back to being Herman Milquetoast as soon as he calms down?"

"I think it's permanent." Sage took a sip of coffee from a Styrofoam cup. "I've seen it in jail inmates. They finally realize that sometimes you have to get tough or you die."

"Will Raymond be prosecuted?" Edward nibbled at a carbonized chicken leg.

"Doubt it. Bigman's presence here has been treated like a state secret. I don't think his father's apt to file a report that could get in the papers."

"Mr. Sage!" David looked up and the ward clerk, a willowy young woman with dark hair to her waist, was at the day room door. "Could you come here a minute, please?"

The clerk was behind the nurses' counter again by the time Sage walked from the day room. "Yes?" he asked.

"There's a lady at the front door to visit you. I told her you were having lunch, but she insisted that you'd want to see her."

"What's her name?"

"Roberta Smith."

"I don't know a Roberta Smith," Sage said. "Besides, only a couple of people know I'm here and you already have their names."

"I don't know about that. But she called from the phone outside and she's very persistent. There's an orderly outside the door waiting on the dietary people to come after the tray cart. Why don't you just walk down and look out. If it's somebody you know, he'll open the door for her."

Puzzled, Sage walked down the long, glistening tiled hallway that was mopped and buffed first thing every morning before the patients got up. Jamey wouldn't give a fictitious name. Lori wouldn't be here at this time of day during the week because the staff knew her.

He stepped up to the door and looked out through the small window of safety glass with wire sandwiched in between the layers. For a moment he thought he was having a waking nightmare.

Lyda Herrel stood a few feet from the door in a yellow gingham dress that fell over her huge body like a circus tent. Her eyes, buried in flesh, were gleaming brightly. Sage opened his suddenly dry mouth to speak, but nothing came out.

The obscenely fat woman reached into a paper bag she was carrying and held something up. It took the detective a moment to focus. *It was a pair of pink booties!* She dangled them like a fishing trophy, smiling, then mouthed the words, *For you, Detective Sage.*

Sage erupted. "Open the door! Open the door, now!"

The orderly, sitting by the door reading a newspaper, stood up, a puzzled look on his face as Sage clawed at the door and screamed again. "Open the door! *Let me out!*"

Sage stepped back and kicked at the double doors, jarring himself all the way to his neck, then slammed at the center with his shoulder, again and again. Lyda Herrel waved cheerily, then turned to walk away.

"Let me out! She's getting away!"

"Mr. Sage, get away from the door!" the orderly demanded.

"The bitch from hell is getting away. Let me out! I have to end this *now*."

"Get away from the door, Mr. Sage. You know I can't let you out," the orderly on the other side of the door declared. It would have taken a bulldozer to open the safety doors. There was no chance that Sage could force them, but the orderly was keeping Sage's attention focused on him as two other orderlies and Nurse Grady, a hypodermic in hand, approached from behind.

The burly orderlies had him by the arms before he knew it. Nurse Grady stepped in with the hypodermic. "Don't do it!" Sage yelled hoarsely. "I've got to put an end to this. Let me out before she gets away!"

"It'll be all right, David," Nurse Grady said as she plunged the needle into his arm and slowly administered the sedative. He continued to struggle briefly, then began to fade away.

"Put him in his bed," Nurse Grady said.

"Restraints?" one of the orderlies asked.

"No, that won't be necessary. He'll be all right after he sleeps awhile. Mr. Sage is a very controlled man. Something horrible must have set him off."

The orderly on the other side of the double doors punched in the security combination, and the door's electronic lock opened.

"I don't know what happened. There was a fat woman out here with a pair of pink booties, and Mr. Sage went berserk."

Lyda Herrel stepped off the elevator on the ground floor, still smiling to herself. She had always known that David Sage was one of the weaklings of the world. Her triumph was just beginning. She waddled across the lobby to the gift shop, getting looks of humor and derision.

"Excuse me," she said to the volunteer clerk behind the counter.

"Yes?" The elderly woman smiled.

"I need to return these booties."

"Something wrong with them?"

"No. It's a terrible thing. My friend that I bought them for lost her little girl during the night. The baby died."

"I'm so sorry," the elderly lady said, taking the receipt. "What a tragedy."

"It really was," Lyda said. "She very much wanted that baby."

"You know," the elderly clerk said, "sometimes it seems that people who don't deserve babies have them and those who really want them, lose them."

"Ain't that the truth," Lyda said as the woman handed her money back.

The clerk watched, sadness in her eyes as Lyda went over to the card section and began to open them one at a time. *A very caring person*, the clerk thought.

In five minutes or so, Lyda was back at the counter with a get well card. On the outside it said: "*Into every life a little rain must fall.*" When opened, there was a picture of a man being drenched by water from a bucket and the words: "*But it seems you've been getting more than your share! Buy an umbrella, dummy!*

The clerk rang up the card, thinking that it seemed inappropriate for a woman who had just lost a baby. But she supposed that the huge woman in the yellow dress knew her friend well enough to choose a card.

"I'll need a first-class stamp," Lyda said. "And may I borrow your pen for a minute?"

SIXTEEN

Private Gordon Platt, the melted man, sat combing his hair as he watched the other prisoners of war around him. The dancing woman sailed by, eyes almost closed and with a smile on her face. Apparently things were desperate for the American war effort. When Gordon had first become a recruit, women hadn't gone into combat. *Obviously things had changed.*

The woman with the purple handkerchiefs stood at a table, flipping through a magazine, hopping from one foot to the other. The effeminate man, who had just been released back into the day room, the one with the pastel cigarettes, and the draft-dodging hippy were playing cards.

Lieutenant Jeeter, the black executive officer who no longer did his job and fraternized with enlisted personnel, was sitting at a table drinking chocolate milk. Jeeter's eyes turned toward the effeminate man once in a while, but mostly he was intently studying the young girl, probably a student nurse. He had watched the effeminate man the same way before Gordon had seen them having sex—disgusting, even if Jeeter hadn't been an officer.

Hardly anybody paid any attention to Gordon, but he saw *everything.* Sergeant Clark was sleeping. The communist keepers had given him a shot after he became upset. The sergeant was a man to watch. Gordon was convinced that Clark was a counterintelligence officer. How else would you explain his ability to slip in and out of the camp? And he was definitely a man who was used to being obeyed.

A nurse and a female aide came in and got the young girl with the violet eyes. They bathed her in the women's bathroom every evening after visitation and got her into night clothes. Lieutenant Jeeter watched them until they were out of the day room, like a beast watching its prey. Jeeter had obviously turned into a renegade officer, a disgrace to his uniform.

The thin, effeminate man got up from his table and went over to Lieutenant Jeeter's table. The black officer winced slightly as the man took a chess set off Jeeter's table and gave him a hard, disrespectful look. Something had definitely happened there. Before, the thin man with the pastel cigarettes had been terrified of Jeeter. Now it almost seemed the other way around.

"Has anyone seen my wife?"

The little bald man stumbled into the day room, a look of horror on his face. His wife had only left an hour or so earlier, but he never seemed to remember. The quality of recruits was definitely going down, Gordon decided.

"Has anyone seen my wife?" The little man stumbled into a chair, hooked his foot on the chrome leg and fell flat on his face. Blood splattered everywhere and pandemonium broke out.

"Jesus!" an orderly yelled through the day room door. "Get some help in here. Mr. Yow just busted his face, and there's blood everywhere!"

In a moment Mr. Yow was surrounded by nurses and orderlies, including the ones who had been bathing the young girl with the violet eyes. They rolled him over and sat him up. He was coughing and gurgling as blood poured from his nostrils.

"Call the ER," one of the nurses yelled to nobody in particular. "I think he's broken the bones around his sinus cavities."

Nobody else noticed as Lieutenant Jeeter got up from his table and slipped out the door, but Private Gordon Platt did. Gordon immediately got up and went into the hallway. The black lieutenant casually walked by the front desk, then by the women's bathroom where the young girl was. He glanced in, looked in both directions, then stepped in and closed the door.

Gordon ran down the hall to Sergeant Clark's room. *It was about time somebody put an end to Lieutenant Jeeter's disgraceful behavior.*

"Sergeant Clark, wake up."

From a sedative-induced distance, David Sage heard the voice. He had been sleeping since they had injected him that afternoon.

"Hurry, Sergeant! Lieutenant Jeeter has the young nurse with the pigtails alone in the bathroom!"

I didn't take long for it to click. Sage bolted up and almost fell over the side of the bed. "Bigman has Rachel in the bathroom? Is that what you're saying?"

"Yes, whatever he calls himself. Hurry, Sergeant!"

"Where are the nurses and orderlies?" Sage asked.

"Never mind that," Gordon said. "*Just hurry!*"

Sage got up, unsteady on his feet, and followed the scarred Gordon down the hall, trying to shake the fog from his mind.

"Don't tell him I'm the one who told you!" Gordon begged as they got to the bathroom door. The melted man hurried on down the hall.

Sage turned the knob and pushed the door open. There were no locked rooms on 6 North, at least none patients could lock from inside. The air was filled with steam and the floor tiles were wet.

"Just stay still, Sweet Cheeks," Sage heard Clifford Bigman say as he tried to hold the girl in place and get his trousers down at the same time. Rachel's legs were apart, one on each side of the old bathtub. "You're gonna *love* this. You'll be *beggin'* me to do it again when I'm finished. Stay still!"

Clifford Bigman had lifted the naked girl upright. He was trying to prop her up against the wall on the edge of the bathtub, but she kept sliding down. Sage could see her eyes, staring over Bigman's shoulder. They held the same expression as when she was being fed or when her father sat beside her weeping. She was in a place where nothing could hurt her.

David Sage was suddenly wide awake. Rage burned through him like the blue-white flame of an acetylene torch as it slices though steel. Assuming a balanced stance, he drove his fist into Clifford Bigman's kidney.

There was a split-second delay between the kidney punch and the roar of rage and pain that came from Bigman as he turned loose of the girl and stood straight up, reaching around to grab his lower back. Rachel began to slide down the wall, and Sage grabbed her under the arms to keep her head from striking the hard ceramic floor. He eased her down on her back. One of her legs stayed over the side of the bathtub, leaving her legs splayed open and vulnerable. Before Sage could lower her leg, Bigman screamed and brought both his fists down on the back of the detective's head.

"*You peckerwood motherfucker! I'm gonna kill you!*"

Sage saw the proverbial stars as Bigman's doubled fist landed on the back of his head, but he was already moving.

Personal combat is not a choreographed affair, but a blur of motion and sound. The detective grabbed Clifford Bigman by the crotch and squeezed hard.

"Ahhhhh . . . ," Bigman screamed, falling back over the tub in an effort to get away. He caught himself on one arm, splashing warm water everywhere. He put out his right arm to stop Sage, and the focused officer caught the huge hand, and with a swift, deliberate motion turned it in on itself. There was a sound like the cracking of kindling wood as bones broke.

The pain was so overwhelming that Bigman couldn't even scream as Sage caught him by the front of his white T-shirt and jerked him to his feet. And the fear! Fear such as Clifford Bigman had never known began to choke him. *So this was how his victims had felt.*

The enraged cop swung Bigman around and shoved him into the hallway. The momentum carried Clifford to the opposite wall. All he wanted to do was get away. Before he could move, though, Sage kicked his kneecap. Cartilage and bone gave way, and Bigman screamed again.

"Arrrrhh . . . Oh God! *Somebody help me!*" the tall, powerful young man yelled.

"Mr. Sage! Stop it right now!" one of the ward nurses yelled from a seemingly faraway place.

Sage stepped in, holding Clifford Bigman against the wall to keep him from collapsing. Bigman could feel the short, stocky officer's breath on the lower part of his face. "I'm going to kill you, Clifford. I'm going to drive your nose up into your brain, and there's not a damn thing you can do to stop me. *How does it feel to be afraid?*"

"Mr. Sage, stop it! For God's sake, I need help around here!" the nurse screamed.

Holding Clifford Bigman against the wall with his left

hand, Sage positioned his feet and brought his right hand back, palm outward. What David Sage knew about combat, he had learned in various places—survival schools, dojos, during military training—but mostly on the streets. His palm shot forward and upward to drive splinters of bone into Clifford Bigman's brain. He would have done it, too, had the orderly not charged in and partially deflected the blow. As it was, only cartilage gave way. Bigman screamed one final time, then passed out.

Sage put his hands up as the big orderly with the ponytail approached him. "I'm all right. It's over. Check on Rachel. He was trying to rape her."

The second-shift nurse, a short, round woman with hair a shade of red found only in a bottle, stepped into the bathroom. Then she glanced down at Clifford Bigman as another nurse tried to stem the bleeding from his nose.

"Get Rachel off the floor, and get a robe on her," the nurse said to the orderly who was facing Sage. "And somebody call the ER and tell them we need *two* gurneys instead of one."

"Don't you want Mr. Sage restrained?" the big blond orderly asked.

"No," the nurse said with a look of disgust at the bleeding Clifford Bigman.

SEVENTEEN

The phone rang as Lloyd Bigman was about to get in bed. He answered it irritably, "Lloyd Bigman."

"Boss, sorry to bother you, but Clifford has been hurt."

"How badly and how?"

"He'll live, but he's been badly beaten by another patient—a county detective. Looks like Clifford was trying to rape a young female patient."

"How far has the paper trail gone?" Bigman asked.

"Right now, hospital security has a report, but they've called for a Horton Police Department investigator because of the brutal nature of Clifford's injury."

"I'll be there in a few minutes." He hung up the phone, went to the closet, and began dressing. Lillith came from the bathroom, a towel around her head. She was wearing a fluffy terry cloth robe.

"Where are you going?" she asked.

"Have to put out a fire," he said.

"Is the congressman drunk again?" she asked.

"No. It's something else. I'll be back as soon as it's handled."

"All right, Lloyd. I'll see you when you get back." She

knew it was futile to pursue the matter when he did not want to talk about it. He kissed her on the cheek and left, as he had done so many times since becoming the right hand of a congressman with a propensity to drink and drive.

In the basement garage Lloyd Bigman started the white Cadillac and punched the remote control to open the door. He looked in the glove box and found a crumpled Marlboro pack with one cigarette in it, pausing long enough to light the cigarette with the car lighter before backing out of the garage.

Sometimes, no, *often*, Lloyd Bigman wondered what he had done to displease God. An angry God seemed to be the only explanation for what had befallen him and his wife. They had both worked hard, given Clifford all the advantages they were able and given 10 percent of their gross earnings to the church since their marriage, even in the days when they struggled to pay the rent. Still, Clifford, the fruit of his loins, was a monster who grew worse as time passed.

If not an angry God, then what? Their tall, strapping son had been normal, or had *seemed* so, right up until the time they had found the naked photographs of Lillith. After it was out in the open, the boy hadn't even tried to hide his twisted yearnings. Lloyd understood that Clifford hardly feared him at all these days. It was only a matter of time until there was a violent conflict between the two.

A God-fearing man with principles, Lloyd knew that his son was beyond redemption and that he and Lillith were responsible for all the damage that Clifford had inflicted on others in recent years. Lloyd had accepted the responsibility, but he knew it had to end before somebody died trying to deter Clifford's bizarre behavior.

Lloyd slowed and turned into the driveway to Municipal Hospital. Around back, he pulled into a space behind the emergency room. A uniformed security officer walked toward the car. He was about to tell Lloyd that no parking was allowed—until he saw the congressional tag on the Cadillac. He merely nodded.

"Over here, Boss," Tim Rumsfield called from the front desk as Lloyd entered the emergency room. "Clifford's in trauma room three. The police department investigator is already back there." Lloyd nodded and walked through the swinging doors without stopping.

Clifford lay sedated on a gurney. His nose was packed with surgical gauze, his right arm was swollen and splinted, and his knee swollen hideously. A short blond hospital security officer was talking to a wiry, young black man with a shaved head, wearing a dark polyester suit from J.C. Penney's, presumably the city investigator. He looked at Lloyd, nodded, and spoke.

"Good evening, Mr. Bigman."

Lloyd extended his hand. "Do I know you, Officer . . ."

"*Investigator* Ahmed Jones." He shook Lloyd's hand firmly. "I heard you speak at the Littlejohn Community Center once. This is Officer James, hospital security." He nodded toward the blond security officer.

"I understand we had a minor incident here involving my son," Lloyd said, also shaking the blond officer's hand.

The investigator's eyebrows shot up. "I'd hardly call it *minor*. A Horton County detective who's a patient on the ward almost killed your son with his bare hands. That's called felonious assault, Mr. Bigman."

Lloyd stared into the investigator's eyes, wondering if he was Muslim or Baptist. Either way, there would be a strong sense of right and wrong to overcome, a streak of puritanical fervor.

"Investigator Jones, I'm sure you already know the embarrassment this would cause me if it became public. And I'm sure you've already been told what instigated the detective to give Clifford an apparently *thorough* beating. . . ."

"Yessir, I'm aware of both factors. Nonetheless . . ."

"Let me finish," Bigman interrupted.

"All right." The investigator's dark face had taken on a stubborn look. Cops don't like political pressure, no matter who is doing the pushing.

"It is my wish that this incident be handled within the confines of this hospital. I will deal with the administrators involved and handle any questions that come your way as a result of not filing a report. Afterward, I'll see that Clifford is never a threat to anyone else."

"Mr. Bigman, I can't do that," the officer said with determination. "There has been at least one felony committed here, maybe two."

"Would you excuse us, Officer James?"

"Sure." The blond security officer walked away, relieved to be out of the loop.

"Investigator Jones, I appreciate your situation, but here's the bottom line. You can walk away with no repercussions, winning my eternal goodwill, or I can call the mayor, who needs the black vote to stay in office, and he'll call your chief, who will probably show up in person. If you still decide to go to a judge for a warrant, the judge probably won't sign it. If he should sign it, a bigger judge will make it go away. Are we clear?"

The investigator swallowed hard, thinking the situation through. After a few moments he decided not to fight the powers-that-be. "Okay, Mr. Bigman. But if this comes back on me, I'll sing to the press like a mockingbird."

"Thank you," Lloyd said. "A young man with your wisdom should go far in the police department. Let me know if I can ever be of assistance."

The angry young cop didn't respond. He turned and left the hospital stiffly with all the dignity of a young wolf cub who has just been put in its place by the pack Alpha male.

❧

David Sage was caught in the dream again. The wooden door had swung open to reveal the beautiful pink-tipped young woman. The red laser-like eyes glowed from both sides. He opened his mouth to scream, not wanting to see the ripped and shredded face for the hundredth time—

"David, wake up! You're having a nightmare."

His eyes popped open, relief flooding through his body.

"Must have been a bad one, Lovah."

"It was," Sage said, sitting up in the bed and reaching for a cigarette.

Jamey picked up the pack, lit two and handed him one. He took a deep drag and exhaled slowly. "You didn't come by yesterday?"

"Well, Lovah," she said in her lower Boston accent, "I have to spend *some* time with my husband. He *expects* it." She laughed her deep, throaty laugh, then leaned over and kissed him on the mouth. "How are you doing?"

"There was a lot of excitement yesterday. I think I'll be well soon."

"*Excuse me?*"

Jamey turned and saw Lori, standing at the door, looking very official in her blue-striped uniform and white apron, a determined expression on her face.

"Yes?" Jamey asked.

"I'll have to ask you to step out of the room while I draw Mr. Sage's blood."

Jamey looked at David from the corner of her almost almond eyes and smiled knowingly. "Of course," she said, putting out her cigarette in the tin ashtray. "I just had a minute anyway. There's someplace I need to be. I'll leave you in the care of your not-so-delicate southern belle, Lovah."

"Thank you," Lori replied, her pale complexion flushing slightly as Jamey walked out.

"Think nothing of it, honey," Jamey answered over her shoulder.

Lori waited until she was sure Jamey was gone, then leaned over and kissed Sage, lingering a few moments as if savoring the experience. "How are you, my hero?"

"Beg pardon?" Sage said.

"Everyone's talking about it this morning. You saved a young girl from being raped."

Sage took a drag from his cigarette. "Probably will cost me my job."

"You prevented a rape, and you'll lose your job?"

"The department doesn't know I'm here. I almost killed the son of a prominent man. I don't think this one can be covered up."

"Everything will work out," Lori said. "I know it will." She whipped the rubber hose around his arm and tapped for a vein. In a couple of minutes she was finished, his morning blood sample safe in her basket.

"I'll call you tonight," she said.

"All right. I'll be expecting it."

Lori paused at the door and stepped aside to let a large, well-dressed black man pass her. "Excuse me," she said.

Lloyd Bigman walked to the side of David Sage's bed and stood there. He emanated power.

"You're Detective David Sage?"

"Yes, sir." Sage put out his cigarette and sat up on the side of the bed, wearing only pajama bottoms, then lit another.

"Doctor tells me you broke Clifford's wrist, damaged a kidney, destroyed one of his knees, and smashed his nose so badly that they've had to reshape it. That was a quite a beating. . . . May I?" Lloyd Bigman took one of Sage's unfiltered Lucky Strikes, picked up the butane lighter, and lit it. He took a deep drag. "I miss smoking, but Lillith is very emphatic about her dislike for it."

"Would you like to sit down, Mr. Bigman?"

"Thank you." The large ebony man with the silver mustache and hair and impeccable clothes pulled a chair up to the bed and sat down. "Now, about my son. That was a severe beating you gave him."

"I meant to kill him, but an orderly deflected the last punch," Sage said.

"Why?" Bigman took another long drag. "You're not a bigot are you?"

"I don't think so. I did it because your son's evil."

"Not *sick*, but *evil*, you say? That's a theological word, not a legal term."

"That's true. But I know evil, and evil has won just one time too often in my life," Sage replied. "I decided to take a stand."

"I see," Bigman said, tapping ashes from his cigarette into the throwaway ashtray on the bedside table. "So last night you were willing to throw away your career—a distinguished one, I checked—to keep evil from winning again?"

"Well, obviously I wasn't thinking with all my faculties. But that's about the size of it."

"A man of principle who actually understands that there's really evil in the world. It's hard to believe, but I have to believe it. May I have another one?"

"Sure," Sage said, handing him a cigarette. "What about you, Mr. Bigman. Do you believe in evil?"

"Yes, I do. Call me Lloyd, Detective Sage." He lit the fresh cigarette and inhaled deeply, held it a minute then let it escape. "Unfortunately, I didn't take definitive action when I should have. But it's hard when your own flesh and blood is involved. And it's not going to be easy on Lillith. She's his mother, even after what he's tried to do to her all these years. I have behaved in a cowardly manner, but I'm about to do what I should have done seven years ago."

"What's that, Mr. . . . Lloyd?"

"Clifford is going down to Nashville, to the hospital for the criminally insane. You familiar with it?"

"Yes, sir. I've delivered prisoners there on several occasions."

"As for the beating you gave Clifford last night—it didn't happen. For your sake, I'm glad you didn't kill him. For Lillith's sake, it would have been better if you had."

"Sir, I don't think the incident can be covered up. Too many people saw it, and hospital security came up here and did a report."

"Detective, I don't think you have any idea how powerful a United States congressman is. I am the right hand *and* brain of such a man. In the past, worse things have gone away. It's not right, but it's true. There is absolutely no record that you sent Clifford to the emergency room last night. People may talk, but it will just be rumors."

"Thank you," Sage said, extending his hand.

"No, *thank you*, Detective, for giving me the courage to do what I should have done a long time ago. I'll be going now to make arrangements, then tell Lillith what happened and arrange for Clifford's commitment. When sufficient time has passed, a letter will be added to your file thanking you for an unspecified piece of work for the congressman. Meanwhile, if you get any heat at all for *anything,* call me. Here's my private number." Lloyd Bigman handed Sage a business card.

After the congressional chief of staff left, Sage lit another cigarette and smoked it slowly. Then he got up and dressed as the breakfast trays went past his door on the noisy food cart. He walked to the day room and drew himself a fresh cup of coffee.

Taking a sip, he turned and saw Mr. Yow sitting quietly at a table. His nose was taped, and he was breathing through his mouth. *Looks like his nose has been broken and packed,* Sage thought. Sage saw Edward and Raymond, trays in front of them, talking as he approached the food cart to pick up his own tray.

"Good morning, Mr. Policeman," a cheery voice said.

Sage stopped and turned toward the sound of the voice. It was Rachel. She was eating, and her eyes were alert and sparkling.

"Breakfast is wonderful this morning. I feel like I've been asleep for a month," the girl with violet eyes said. "Would you sit with me this morning?"

"I'd be delighted to have breakfast with you, Rachel," Sage replied, wondering when *his* time of healing would come.

"What are you gonna do with all this gasoline, Lyda?" Rafe Herrel asked as his daughter carried in the last of four ten-gallon cans from the pickup truck.

"I'm going to mow the front pasture down to the road tomorrow, and I don't want to run out of gas." She put down the ten-gallon can inside the basement door and wiped her hands on the sides of a huge pair of bibbed overalls worn over a black T-shirt.

"*One* can would have mowed the whole front pasture. Besides, I was gettin' ready to turn the heifers down into that field to graze it down." He wiped his forehead with a blue-and-white bandanna. His overalls were the same kind as Lyda's, but ten sizes smaller. Even at that they still hung on his nearly cadaverous frame.

"Then the silly fucking cows can just eat it dry off the ground!" Lyda's voice rose in pitch and volume.

"Now, Lyda, don't get fired up. I'm just tryin' to tell ya that the front pasture don't need to be mowed. It's a waste of time and energy."

"All my life you've been belittling me!" She was almost screaming, her face mottled and red. "I try to do something good, and you make fun of me. If I'd been born with a pecker things would have been different, wouldn't they? The sign out there would have said "Herrel and Son" by now. And you wouldn't even take care of my rottweilers while I was gone! Nothing I ever did pleased you."

"Lyda, them dogs was beyond me. I just couldn't . . ." Rafe Herrel was retreating slowly when the storm door on the back porch came open. He had hoped to be somewhere else before his wife was drawn into the fracas. She lumbered onto the back porch.

"What's wrong, Lyda?" She glanced at her husband. "What's your daddy done to you now?"

"It's the same old thing, Mama. I try to do something nice, and he gets all over me." Tears were rolling down Lyda's moon face.

"All I said was"—Rafe took a deep breath, knowing his protests were useless—"that she didn't need all that gas to mow the front pasture—and it don't need mowin' anyway!"

"That girl never has been able to please you, Rafe. You always wanted a boy, and you let her know it."

Rafe Herrel waved them off with his hand, then walked away in disgust. He knew there was no talking to either one of them.

"Lyda, you do whatever you think is right. I'm makin' biscuits and gravy for breakfast. I cooked a whole pound of bacon for you. Soon as you're through, come on in and eat. I guess your daddy'll be off sulkin'. I opened you a fresh jar of honey, too."

"Thanks, Mama. I'll be right there." Lyda watched her mother waddle back into the house. *Silly old bitch,* she thought to herself. *You ain't no smarter than he is, and you love this worthless farm as much as he does. But that's going to change very soon. Very soon.*

EIGHTEEN

"Well, Mr. Sage. I see there's been a lot of excitement around here while I've been gone." Dr. Wohlford was back. Wherever he had been, it was not a place where sunshine had gotten to him. He was as pale as when he left, and his Adam's apple was bobbing at full speed.

"Yes, there has," Sage responded, taking a sip of coffee at the day room table where they were sitting.

"I understand you hurt another patient?" Wohlford put the unlit briar pipe in his mouth and sucked on it, waiting for an explanation.

"He was trying to rape a little girl in the bathroom. I was helping her. Then I had to defend myself."

"That's what the nurse on duty said. She didn't order you restrained or sedated," the doctor noted. "But Mr. Bigman's injuries were extensive. Wasn't there some kind of police judo or something you could have used without doing all that damage?"

"No," Sage replied. "It doesn't work that way."

"But you *were* sedated earlier when an unexpected visitor showed up. Would you like to tell me about it?"

"It was a woman I sent to prison. Her conviction was overturned and she somehow found out I was here. She showed up to taunt me, and I just lost it for a moment."

"Are you still having hallucinations?"

"If you mean the savior, the answer is yes." Sage saw that Gaynel was dancing near the television at the back of the room where Dr. Chavez Wilson was attempting to speak to the old sailor, Mr. Beal, without success. Katrina stood nearby, dancing from foot to foot. She worried every day that Dr. Wilson would start force-feeding her.

"I'm going to up your dosage a little and we'll see what happens in a couple of days," Wohlford said, scratching something on his clipboard. He unfolded himself from the table and turned to the back of the room where Gaynel was gliding across the floor.

"Mr. Sage, you have a telephone call," an orderly said from the day room door. "It's your sister."

As Sage went out into the hall, Dr. Chavez Wilson moved over to Gaynel and told her to sit down. She did so reluctantly, leaning her head back and closing her eyes.

Dr. Wohlford approached and put his hand out to his fellow psychiatrist. "Dr. Wilson. I see that you're taking over Gaynel's care."

"I hope you understand that I didn't solicit the change. Mrs. Potts's husband approached me," Wilson explained.

"Of course," Wohlford replied. "I never thought otherwise. I certainly haven't done a bang-up job with her."

Gaynel sat as they discussed her, seemingly uninterested, head still back.

"Well, you have apparently reached the limits of chemical therapy," Wilson said.

"Then you'll be going with ECT?"

"Yes, first thing in the morning," Wilson replied.

"Gaynel," Wohlford said, "do you understand that Dr. Wilson is now your physician and you'll be starting something new tomorrow in the way of treatment? You may be out of here soon if it works."

"My son, I'll be out of here when the heavenly Father decides that I have done what I was sent to do," Gaynel said in her deep, melodious voice.

Somewhat startled, Wilson asked, "And what were you sent here to do, Gaynel?"

"To set at liberty those who are in bondage. To forgive their sins." She turned a watery stare from behind the thick glasses toward the doctors, then stood and whirled away.

"Do you think she understood anything we said?" Wilson asked his colleague.

"Don't know." Wohlford sucked on his unlit pipe and watched Gaynel dance by David Sage as he walked back into the day room.

Lori Henderson hung up her pale pink Princess telephone, a smile on her face. Her breasts were small and her hips didn't draw the kind of attention that Jamey's did, but David Sage wasn't a shallow man bowled over by opulent flesh. He was sensitive and brave and Lori was in love, though she hadn't quite admitted it to herself. She hugged the sheriff's department yearbook, just as Sandra came by, toweling herself off from a shower.

"You've been talking to your crazy cop again, haven't you?" Sandra stood there tall and striking in unashamed nudity, drying the insides of her thighs.

"Yes, I have." Lori averted her eyes. An only child, modesty had been a big deal at her house. Even after two years, she had not grown used to Sandra's carefree attitude about bare skin.

"Did you let him fuck you last weekend?"

"*No!*" Lori's pale skin flushed crimson.

"You *did*. My shy, unassuming little country girl let a total stranger into her pants—and on the first date. I wish I'd been here last weekend to protect you." Sandra stood, hands on hips, staring in mock surprise.

"It wasn't like that. I didn't *let* him do anything. I seduced him, and we made love together. *That's* what happened!"

Sandra came in and sat on the bed, her long, cone-shaped breasts bounced as she sank into the mattress. "Lori, how old is this David Sage?"

"He's around forty, but he looks a lot younger."

"When you're forty, he'll be *fifty-six*. Have you thought about that?"

"I haven't thought about anything else *except* David Sage in days."

"Honey, I just hope you know what you're doing."

"All I know," Lori answered fiercely, "is that when he walks out of that ward, I'll be there waiting for him!"

"Do I need to find a new roommate?"

"I don't know. We haven't discussed it yet."

"I wanted to stop and say good-bye."

Sage looked up and saw Raymond standing by the table, wearing a sports jacket and dress slacks and holding a small travel bag.

"Your doctor's releasing you?"

"No, I'm signing myself out."

"Are you sure about this?" Sage asked, lighting a cigarette.

"Yes, I am. I've realized that there are no easy solutions. Watching you has made me realize that whatever my solutions are, I have to find them myself. It's time for me to stop doing what I've accused Edward of—hiding in here. I don't know if I'm a gay man or a straight man, but I *am* a man. All I had to do was say it and *mean* it."

"Raymond, I'm hiding in here," Sage quietly said.

"No you're not. You're *waiting* on something. I don't know what it is, but you do. When it happens, you'll be back out there protecting people and solving crimes."

"I appreciate your confidence, Raymond. Have you talked to Edward yet?"

"I will on the way out." Raymond extended his hand and Sage shook it firmly.

"Good luck, Raymond."

"I don't need luck, just courage. I'm going to finish law school. I'll see you in court in a year or so, Detective." He turned and walked toward the door, shoulders back.

"I don't doubt that at all, Raymond," Sage said quietly as Raymond left the day room.

"You talking to yourself now, David?" Larry Ware asked, plopping his large bulk into one of the folding chairs at the card table.

"How did you get in here, Partner? It's not time for evening visitors."

"Flashed my badge and gave 'em my best smile. Showed pearly whites and pink gums. Nobody can resist my Little Black Sambo smile. If I liked watermelon and blondes I could slide through this world as a stereotype."

"I thought you *did* like blondes. You want some coffee, Larry?"

"I do like blondes, but I don't want to make you white boys nervous. That coffee as good as jail coffee? If it is I'll have a cup—black."

Ware sat and looked around while his partner drew two cups from the urn on the table by the door. In a minute Sage was back. He sat two Styrofoam cups on the table.

"You ain't getting accustomed to this place are you, David? I can see how it would be easy. No taxes, no police, nobody to bother you."

Gaynel glided through the door on tiptoes. She swirled past the two detectives, stopping long enough to pick up David's coffee. "Thank you, my child."

She danced away again. Without speaking, Sage went and got himself another cup of coffee and returned. "What's wrong with her, the dancer?" Ware asked.

"What makes you think there's anything wrong with her?"

"Well, my detective friend, she obviously ain't a member of the staff, so that makes her a patient. She *must* be suffering from some form of craziness. What is it? I don't see how anybody can keep up that constant movement."

Sage took a sip of coffee. "She says she's the savior."

"As in *Jesus* the Savior?" Ware asked, turning the cup up and swallowing it in two gulps.

"No, not Jesus—but the same thing. Sent here to do God's work."

"David, you haven't overstayed here have you?" Lines formed into a "V" on the forehead of Ware's mahogany face. "You sound like you believe in her."

Sage's face brightened. He shook off his serious expression. "Hang around here a few days, Larry. You might be surprised what you'll come to believe."

They both laughed uneasily.

"You talked to Lloyd Bigman yet?" Ware asked without warning.

"Yeah. How did you know about Bigman?"

"I caught the original case, remember? Took care of the matter. Lloyd called me and asked about you this morning."

"You must have said something he liked. It's all squared away. Clifford is on his way to the forensic unit at Central State."

"Good." The big detective stood up. "I gotta be going, David. For real, when will you be out of here? I don't know how long I can keep shuckin' and jivin' Lieutenant Lardass Bullock."

"Soon, Larry. Very soon, I think."

Sage stood and they shook hands—one large black man, one short, stocky white man. Two cops. Brothers, who would have died for each other.

"Later, David." Larry Ware left the room in large strides, as always in a hurry.

As Sage went to warm up his coffee and get a snack from the little refrigerator, Edward came through the door of the day room, barefoot. His shoulders slumped forward, his silver-streaked hair pulled back into a ponytail.

"Raymond just left. Gone, checked out."

"I know," Sage replied, fishing out a dish of rice pudding with Raymond's name on it. "He decided it was time."

"Well, I for one don't think he was ready. He'll be back in a day or two. Mark my words. Raymond's too delicate."

"No he's not, Edward. He's tough. He just didn't know it before. He'll do just fine." Sage sat down at a table with a plastic spoon and his coffee and took a bite of the rice pudding. It was full of golden raisins, and it was delicious.

"And when are *you* leaving?" Edward asked.

"I don't know. When I'm sav—*healed*. I'll leave when I'm well."

"You started to say *saved*. You think Gaynel Potts really is the savior don't you? If you do, that probably makes you crazier than her!"

David took another bite of rice pudding. "We've had this conversation, Edward. I thought we agreed that if I was crazy I wouldn't know it."

Edward sat down, laying his long, lank arms on the table. "I 'borrowed' a screwdriver from the guy who was working on the vents outside the room."

"What?" Sage paused with a spoonful of pudding almost to his mouth.

"I borrowed—actually, I stole—a screwdriver from the air-conditioning repairman. That's how I got the safety windows out that night. You remember, when I went out on the ledge."

"What did you do with it?"

"It's hidden above the shower stall."

"So why are you telling me now?"

"Because you wanted to know. Besides, they didn't believe me the last time, and I don't think they'll believe me if I do it again. Wohlford says he may kick me out tomorrow."

"Edward, would you like for me to help you get on at the county?"

"The sheriff's department?"

"No. But there are a lot of other jobs. Maintenance work, inside and out. All kinds of stuff. If you're interested, I'll give you my phone number before one of us leaves."

"I guess it's inevitable that I'll have to leave here someday," Edward said, resting his chin on his palms.

"Worse things have happened to people," David Sage observed.

NINETEEN

"That sounds good, honey. If I'm still here Friday, I'll get a pass. *No,* Jamey didn't come back after you left this morning. . . . I don't know *when* she might be back. She doesn't keep a schedule like everyone else."

Sage glanced around to see if anyone was eavesdropping. The patient phone was mounted on the wall across from the nurses' station so that patients could be monitored if they became agitated or were making harassing phone calls. There were no phones in the rooms. Evening visitation had just started, and family members were walking up and down the halls with their loved ones and friends.

"It's getting busy in the hall, Lori. I need to hang up and get out of the way. Okay, I'll see you in the morning. Good night."

Gaynel's John Goodman look-alike husband, George Potts, came down the hall, huge belt buckle shining. He was wearing a Western shirt with mother-of-pearl buttons and Levi's. His cowboy boots were tapping. Sage followed Gaynel's husband into the day room. He wanted to be close, just in case the over-sized lout got violent.

"Damn," he said to himself. The day room was packed with visitors. Gaynel was at the back, dancing in front of the piano. As her husband approached, she seemed to shrink visibly. She made no resistance as the big man motioned for her to sit on the piano bench and took a seat beside her.

"Detective Sage!" Rachel, her violet eyes lively and laughing, her dark hair falling freely down her back, motioned for Sage to come to the table where she was sitting with her father. Sage walked across the room, glancing at Gaynel and her husband. The savior was cowering away from the big man, nodding her head fearfully.

"You're looking very beautiful, Rachel," Sage said.

"Sit with us," she said. "This is my father, John Cunningham. Daddy, this is Detective David Sage. He saved me from the bad man."

Sage looked at the girl, a puzzled expression on his face. "What do you remember, Rachel?" He had hoped that she remembered none of it.

"Just that I was wet and naked and the bad, bad man had me. You made him turn me loose."

"It's all right," John Cunningham said. He was a youthful, fortyish man with gray at the temples. "Dr. Wilson and the head nurse told me what almost happened. I decided it was better to put it all behind Rachel, rather than press charges. She's suffered enough losing her mother. And I'm forever in your debt, Detective." Tears came to the man's eyes as he extended his hand.

"I'm getting out tomorrow," Rachel said. "Will you bring your red-headed girlfriend and visit us?"

"Rachel!" her father said. "You've embarrassed Detective Sage."

"Well, I saw her kiss him when I walked by the door this

morning. I was going to visit him. I saw the girl who takes blood kiss him." She turned to Sage. "That makes her your girlfriend, doesn't it?"

"Maybe, Rachel. But you must not mention that to anyone else. It could get Lori in trouble. And we *will* come and visit you after I get out of here."

"Damn it, Gaynel!" George Potts's voice roared across the room, causing heads to turn. Gaynel had fallen to the floor, pulling away from him on the piano bench. "*This is going to stop!*" Realizing that everyone was looking, he lowered his voice, but not enough. "We'll just see if it doesn't stop. We'll just see what happens *tomorrow*." He turned on the heel of his cowboy boot, almost toppled, then stalked down the hall toward the exit without looking back.

"Wonder what's wrong with him," John Cunningham said.

"He's an illiterate, insensitive redneck," Sage replied.

"Guess you meet a lot of those as a police officer, right, David?" Rachel observed.

Lyda Herrel stood in the basement, surveying the area. Everything was in place. Her liberation was at hand. She had screwed the tops off all four red-and-yellow gasoline cans, and the odor in the basement was almost overpowering.

The old cardboard box of greasy rags that her father always kept, despite her mother's nagging, was a foot from the gasoline cans. *Spontaneous combustion. Everybody knows about spontaneous combustion,* she thought. The police might suspect something, but they wouldn't be able to prove anything.

She felt around in her pockets to make sure the cotton

balls were still there. A couple of them lit by a butane lighter and tossed into the rag box would burn hot, especially with a little gasoline that Lyda would spill on the floor. The cotton balls would be consumed entirely. Let them bring in their dogs to sniff out petroleum products. It wouldn't matter.

"I tried to warn him," Lyda would say with appropriate weeping, "about keeping those old greasy rags and storing gasoline in the basement, but he just wouldn't listen. You know how old people are when their thinking slows down, don't you, Officer? I tried to get them out. Honest to God, I tried. What am I going to do without my mommy and daddy?"

A smile came to Lyda's rotund face as she played the scenario through in her mind. *I'll be driving a new Corvette and living in a nice condo in the city. That's where I'll be without those old fools.*

"Lyda, are you down there?" her mother asked from the top of the basement stairs.

"Yes, Mama. I've been looking for my old high school yearbooks."

"The yearbooks are in the attic," he mother said. "Why is there such a strong smell of gasoline in the basement, Lyda?"

"I guess a little must have spilled when I was bringing it in, Mama."

"Smells like more than a little. Oh well, we can check it tomorrow. Come on up. It's after nine, and five o'clock comes early."

"I don't think you'll be checking anything tomorrow," Lyda muttered under her breath.

"What was that?" her mother asked.

"I said, 'I'm on my way up,' Mama."

∞

"David?"

"Yes, Edward."

"You're smoking in bed again, aren't you?"

"Yes, Edward, I am."

The outside lights filtered eerily through the windows of the double room. Voices murmured from the nurses' station as the night nurse and an orderly chatted quietly. From time to time an air-conditioning unit would start up in a room somewhere up or down the hall.

"David?"

"Yes, Edward?"

"I think I'm going to get a pass tomorrow and go down and get my car started. I'm sure the battery's dead by now."

"I didn't know you had a car here."

"Well, it's not much of a car, but it got me to Horton."

"From where, Edward?"

"Charlotte, North Carolina. I got here with ten dollars in my pocket. I didn't know what to do. Finally, I went out and found a tab of LSD and ate it so I could get in the hospital."

"So, you haven't really been hearing voices?"

"No, it was just a scam."

"Edward, had you ever been here before? In Horton, I mean."

"No. Just drove in the day I came to the hospital."

"How did you score the LSD so quick?"

"Nothing to it, David. I can go into any city in America and buy dope in an hour. It's a talent I have."

Sage ground out his cigarette, then lit another. "Edward, you know when we were talking about a job with the county?"

"Yeah."

"With your talent, the narcotics unit could probably put

you to work tomorrow and front you the money for a place to stay, plus buy groceries."

"You mean narc on other people?"

"Yeah, that's what I mean. You wouldn't have to stay at a mission while you were getting back on your feet."

"How . . . I mean, who would set this up?"

"I've got a buddy—went to the academy with him—who runs the narcotics unit at the sheriff's department. I'll call him, if you want me to."

"You'd do that for somebody you met in a psych ward?"

"Why not, Edward? You're obviously at least as sane as I am."

TWENTY

Larry Ware finished the last of the paperwork on the case that had kept him going since nine-thirty the evening before, and saw that it was four-thirty in the morning. He sighed deeply and put on his size fifty-six-long gray sports jacket and stuffed his necktie in his pocket.

A mentally retarded nineteen-year-old had been found beaten to death beside a country road. The stupidity of his murderer had made the case easy to solve, but no less tiresome. The first thing a homicide detective has to determine is who a victim is, the second is *who* saw him last. Who he was turned out to be no problem since his empty wallet was still on his body. Who saw him last was also easy. The victim, Dwight Polk, had left work with one Juan Lopez from the meat-packing company where they worked. Both had just been paid.

Lopez had welcomed the detective with an innocent smile into his shabby house trailer. He hadn't seen Dwight since the night before, had dropped him off at a bar, he told Ware. The wet spot on the carpet? He had spilled beer there and cleaned it up.

Lopez's smile had vanished when the big detective walked over and turned a plastic lampshade around. The lazy killer had cleaned the blood from the carpet and wiped all the spatters from the wall, but had just turned the lampshade around, bloody side toward the wall. The ball bat with which he had pounded Dwight Polk to a pulp was in a storage room. Lopez had washed the blood off, but there would still be traces for the lab. The stupidity of murderers and other criminals never ceased to amaze Larry Ware.

The big detective locked up, turned off the lights and left. He was parked in Lieutenant Bullock's marked spot in the garage. Sometimes he left it there when he worked all night so he could watch Bullock's pale face get all splotchy when he arrived in the morning.

As he pulled onto the interstate, Ware lit up a rare cigarette. Black men and high blood pressure. His mother reminded him often of the lethal combination. But he loved smoking. He had decided a cigarette once in a while wouldn't kill him.

A few minutes later the detective was in Shagbark, a small community on the outskirts of Horton where even in the days of the approaching millennium black people were rare. That was one reason Larry had chosen an apartment in the community.

Another cop, who had been getting free rent for doing security there, had moved. The owner had asked his tenant to find another cop who might like the same deal. The elderly landlord had kept his composure and hesitated only briefly before handing over the keys. Too big and black to argue with, Larry had laughingly told David Sage, *Nigger usually don't have a badge and a gun.*

"Well," Ware said to himself, "better get my fix of cholesterol before I go home." He wheeled the unmarked cruiser onto the lot of the Waffle House and stopped, looking closely to see who was eating at that time of morning. He didn't see any obvious drunken rednecks and didn't really want to. On several occasions he had jailed patrons for indiscrete comments about "niggers in fancy cars."

Inside he took his regular seat at the very back against the wall where he could watch the door. A skinny waitress with a front tooth missing came over smiling. She said, "Good mornin', Lieutenant Al Giardello."

"Good morning, Shelia." It was an old joke between them. His resemblance to Yaphet Koto, who played an African-Italian homicide lieutenant on the popular television show, *Homicide: Life on the Streets,* was striking. Shelia was an intense fan and she knew the real names of all the characters and could ramble on about every episode because she had taped them all.

"Did ya catch *Homicide* last Friday?"

"No, I was too busy solving a real homicide, Shelia."

"It was good."

"I'm sure it was."

"And it's been good for black people. I'd always thought of black people as different from the rest of us. But you're really not, are you?"

"Well, not *too* different except for a fondness for water-melon and fried chicken."

"You're kiddin' me again, Larry." She grew very serious. "I ain't real smart, but I know when I'm bein' kidded."

"Yup, just a joke, Shelia. I really don't like fried chicken. Bring me coffee, three over easy, toast and a side of bacon and hashbrowns."

"Comin' right up, Gi."

Clad in a pink terrycloth robe, her hair up in large, pink curlers, Lyda carefully made her way down the concrete steps by the light of a small yellow bulb on the back porch. She was going outside to the back garage basement door because the wooden steps inside squeaked too badly. Not that the old fools, snoring like bulldogs, would hear anything. But why take chances?

A beagle from the farm next door, interrupted during his bowel movement, went berserk about twenty feet from Lyda. She clumsily bent over, picked up a handful of gravel and hurled it at the dog. "*Get out of here!*" she hissed.

The dog yelped as the gravel landed around him and headed home at a fast trot. Lyda stood in the moonlight, listening for movement in the house and watching for a light to come on. After a minute, she cautiously made her way to the outside door, which she had left unlocked when she was down there earlier.

The door creaked as she pushed it open, and she reached in and turned on the light. A large spider ran over her foot, causing Lyda to do a cumbersome, hopping dance while holding in a scream. She was afraid of spiders.

"Damn!" she said quietly to herself. "The gas really *does* smell strong in here. Oh well, I'll be away from it in just a minute."

She fished the handful of cotton balls from the right pocket of her robe and a yellow plastic butane lighter from the other pocket. Lyda had never paid much attention to anything when she was in school, especially science class. Otherwise, she might have known about the volatility of gasoline when its fumes permeate the air.

Standing over the rag box, Lyda held up the cotton balls and flicked the lighter. A small flame shot up, igniting the cotton. She dropped the flaming mass. Somewhere between the floor and her hand, the flames met the exact flashpoint of the concentrated fumes.

It happened so quickly that Lyda didn't even scream. There was a loud whoosh as the air ignited, then the gasoline she had spilled on the floor went up along with all of four ten-gallon cans. Lyda's hair ignited almost instantly and the pink curlers turned into a mass of flaming droplets. Her vision was gone almost immediately and the robe burst into flames. The explosion blew the garage doors out into the yard.

Nevertheless, self-preservation carried Lyda almost outside before she went down, sucking in the super-heated air and blistering her lungs into uselessness. She collapsed on the floor, gurgling, and stayed there.

The explosion woke Lyda's parents. They smelled the smoke boiling up the inside stairs and got out of the house, stopping just long enough to dial 911.

"Dispatch to any homicide detective clear for service," the portable radio crackled.

Larry Ware sopped up the last bite of egg yolk with his last bite of toast and put it in his mouth. He was off duty, not on call. If he didn't answer, nobody would know he was still up. The dispatcher would go to the roster and wake somebody else. He chewed thoughtfully, then washed the toast down with hot coffee. "What the hell?" he said to himself. "Who needs sleep?" He picked up the small portable and answered.

"Unit 507, I'm clear."

"House fire with a fatality. Can you see the Rural Metro and the arson investigator at the scene?"

"Ten-four. Give me the address." He jotted down the address, then took out his wallet and left a liberal tip. The management fed cops for free.

"See you later, Shelia," Ware said on his way out.

At least the fire was nearby. There was a chance he would get a little sleep today. He turned up Clifton Road and began to look for a street address on a mailbox. Slowing down as he neared the number, Larry worked his spotlight from side to side. *Herrel Farm.* Lyda Herrel's address!

Ware drove up the gravel driveway to the old farmhouse, and stopped near the flashing red lights of a pumper truck, a first responder vehicle, and an ambulance. Jake Powell, the sheriff's department arson investigator, was talking to a fire captain from Rural Metro. The fire captain shook his head affirmatively and walked over to give instructions to a fire-fighter.

"What's up?" Jake asked as the big homicide investigator approached. A small, wiry man with a face wrinkled beyond his forty years, Powell was dressed like the firemen in a yellow slicker and helmet. Fires were his passion.

"About to ask you the same question, Jake." The air was filled with the smell of burnt wood and smoke, but there was something else, another odor in the air, like bacon frying.

"Gasoline explosion, about twenty gallons, I think. In the garage. There's a pile of hot suet just inside, still too hot to examine. Parents say it's their daughter, Lyda Herrel, age thirty."

"Parents around?" Ware asked.

"No, had to take the old lady to the hospital, and the old man went with her. She collapsed when we found the body. Probably caused about four hernias being lifted into the ambulance. Real whale." Jake lit a cigarette and took a drag.

"How'd it happen, Jake?"

"Well, the parents think she was down here trying to fight the fire."

"Was she?"

"Nope, she was torching the place. No doubt about it. Her father said she had carried in gasoline that she didn't need earlier. Nobody smokes, but there's what's left of a yellow butane lighter on the floor. Another genius strikes in the middle of the night. She didn't even do a lot of damage. Fire trucks were on the scene in a few minutes. Nothing hurt but the garage—and her big lardass."

"You know, Jake. Sometimes God pulls his own sting operations, even when the criminal justice system drops the ball. Right now, Lyda Herrel is probably being issued her uniform in hell."

Jake just stared at Larry and said nothing.

TWENTY-ONE

David Sage opened his eyes as Lori came into the room. It had been a bad night. The glowing red eyes and the mutilated young woman had come twice. He was still soaked in sweat from the last dream.

"You're early," he said.

"Someone called in sick. I have two extra floors today. Why are you awake so early?" She glanced over at Edward snoring loudly and kissed Sage lightly on the mouth.

"Bad dreams," he said. "Twice."

"Have you talked to your doctor about the dreams?" She put her metal basket on the side of the bed and pulled out the rubber hose.

"No. He can't help me. It's a spiritual matter."

"Oh?" She pulled the band around his arm and tightened it.

"You don't think highly of psychiatrists do you?" She tapped until she located a vein, then smoothly slipped in the needle.

"Only to hand out prescriptions. I never believed that an eighteenth-century doctor, living in a small Jewish community in Vienna, ever arrived at any universal truths."

"Well, Freud was just the beginning. That's what they told

me in college." He kissed her on the cheek as she bent forward, inhaling honeysuckle and isopropyl alcohol.

"David! You'll cause me to collapse a vein." The blood flowed quickly into the tube. She removed the needle and slapped a Band-Aid over the puncture.

"Do you still want to see me this weekend?" he asked.

"Of course I do. I want you every weekend." She blushed deeply. "When are you going to leave here?"

"When I'm well. When the dreams go away."

"When do you think that will be?" She put her tools back in the wire basket.

"Maybe tomorrow, maybe today. I don't know."

She leaned over and kissed him again, then left quickly. After she was gone, Sage sat up and retrieved a cigarette and lighter from the bedside table.

"Do all cops have beautiful women in love with them?" Edward asked.

"Edward, you're a snoop. You should have let us know you were awake." Sage inhaled deeply.

"Well, you don't have much expectation of privacy in a double-bed hospital room," Edward said.

"I guess you're right, Edward." Sage stepped to the floor and hunted for his shoes. He slipped them on without socks and picked up his shirt from the foot of the bed.

"Do they?"

"No, Edward, and I usually don't, either."

"You couldn't prove it by me. I'd take either one you didn't want. That Jamey is a hot-looking woman."

"I'm going to get a cup of coffee, Edward."

"I'll be down in a couple of minutes," he replied.

Dr. Chavez Wilson was at the counter talking to the night nurse. It was apparently ECT day for Mr. Beal and Katrina, though they had not been wheeled into sight yet. The night nurse was the only nurse who actually wore a white uniform and cap to work. Sage had heard her tell someone that she had worked too long for the uniform to leave it at home.

Sage drew himself a hot cup of coffee, which had apparently just been made. It was quiet in the day room. Normally Gaynel was up well before anyone else, but she was nowhere in sight. Sage toyed with the idea of turning on the television for the morning news, but decided it would only depress him more.

Edward padded into the day room, barefoot as usual, and drew a cup of hot coffee. His shoulder-length black and silver hair was in wild disarray. *He will definitely make a good narc,* Sage thought to himself.

The tall, lanky pseudo-hippy pulled out a folding chair and sat down at Sage's table. "Dr. Shocker is here this morning," Edward said. "Before it's over, he's going to have everyone in this ward on electroconvulsive therapy."

"What do you mean?" Sage asked, taking a sip of coffee. "You aren't going to volunteer, are you?"

"Nope, but I see Gaynel is going out for her first treatment today."

"No, Edward. Gaynel is Dr. Wohlford's patient. He doesn't use ECT."

"Gaynel's redneck husband fired Wohlford and hired Wilson. She's sitting at the end of the hall in a wheelchair right now, along with Mr. Beal and Katrina, knocked out and waiting for the people from ECT to come after her. *Where are you going?*"

Sage had turned his chair over getting up. He dashed across the day room and out into the hall. Two orderlies dressed in white and a nurse's aide had the security doors open, preparing to take out Mr. Beal, Katrina, and Gaynel. The alarmed cop sprinted down the hall and stopped. The two men and the woman in white looked up at him in surprise.

"There's been a mistake," Sage said. "Gaynel isn't supposed to have shock therapy."

One of the orderlies, a short, stocky crewcut man of Sage's size and build, looked at the clipboard he was carrying. "I have the order right here. Wanta see it?"

"I don't *need* to see it. You can't do this to her. It'll be like crucifying her again," Sage said. He grabbed the handles to Gaynel's wheelchair and backed away. When the stocky orderly advanced, Sage stepped in front of Gaynel and said, "You don't want to try it. I don't know how bad you think you are, but you really don't want to try to take her."

"What's the problem here?" Sage looked over his shoulder and saw that Dr. Chavez Wilson, hair slicked back and bushy eyebrows lifted, had emerged from a room and was standing there, clipboard in hand. "Mr. Sage, what are you doing?"

"I'm protecting Gaynel, you fucking butcher! You can't take her down to your little shop of horrors and scramble her brains. I won't let you! *You have no idea who she is.*"

"Mr. Sage, I do know who she is. I don't know what kind of silly stories you've heard about ECT treatments, but it's *not* a medieval torture. Gaynel is a very disturbed woman who has not responded to any other therapy. Her husband and I have decided that this is the proper course of treatment. I appreciate that you are a man trained to assist the weak and helpless, but I must insist that you get out of the way and let these people do their jobs."

"No."

"All right"—the doctor nodded at the two orderlies—"move Mr. Sage out of the way."

"I wouldn't try it," Sage said in a quiet voice, as the short, stocky man and his taller, thinner colleague moved toward him.

Both of them halted, looked at each other, then back at Sage.

"Mr. Sage," Dr. Wilson said. "You are an intelligent man. You know you cannot prevent this."

"I'm willing to die trying," the detective replied in a soft voice.

The shorter one dropped his head and charged while he thought Sage was distracted. The cop sidestepped only a fraction of an inch, caught the orderly's wrist and using the man's own momentum, slammed him to the floor, propelling him down the hall past Dr. Wilson on his chest and forearms.

"Shut the door, and call Security from outside," the psychiatrist ordered the nurse's aide. The orderly got up, rubbing his burning palms against the sides of his white trousers.

Sage turned Gaynel's wheelchair around and pushed her past the doctor. Examining the floor burns on his forearms, the stocky orderly stepped warily out of Sage's way. They all followed him at a distance as he wheeled Gaynel into the day room and knelt in front of her wheelchair.

"Gaynel! Gaynel! *Wake up.* They're trying to crucify you again."

"Mr. Sage," Dr. Wilson said from the day room door, "this is your last chance to step away from Gaynel. Two security officers are coming down the hall right now. Just move away and we'll forget this happened."

"No! *Gaynel, wake up!*" Sage shook her, but her head only moved from side to side.

In a moment the two uniformed officers and the two orderlies had David Sage trapped in a half-circle, like wolves approaching their prey. Sage stepped in front of Gaynel's wheelchair and waited, arms loose at his side.

"I think we ought to get another couple of guys," the short orderly with the floor burns said. "He's dangerous."

"Let a *pro* do it, son." One of the security officers, a man in his early twenties, a weightlifter by appearance with curly blond hair, stepped forward, drawing a baton from his belt ring. It was called the PR-24, or "prosecutor." David Sage was an instructor in its use. He was ready when the officer moved.

As expected, the young security officer came in low, spinning the handle in his hand to strike Sage across the shins. Sage stepped into the swing, turning his shoulder toward the security officer. When he stepped back, the PR-24 was in *his* hands, while the officer bent at the waist, gasping for breath from the elbow that had hit his solar plexus.

Sage spun the baton expertly, then brought it alongside his forearm. "You shouldn't *ever* bring a weapon into a ward full of crazy people," Sage said.

Even as he spoke, however, another security officer and two more orderlies joined the group. It would be over quickly, and Sage knew it. Keeping his eyes on all of them, he tried to shake Gaynel awake once more. "Wake up, Gaynel. Wake up. *They're going to crucify you!*"

The third security officer was a sergeant, and Sage recognized him. A retired officer from the Horton City Police Department. "All right," the sergeant said. "We've fucked around long enough. *Swarm him!*"

It was over in less than a minute. Sage didn't swing the baton because he didn't want to hurt anybody. He kept struggling, but to no avail. He felt the restraint straps closing around his arms and legs and heard Dr. Wilson call for an injection. Finally, he lay strapped and unmoving. A nurse approached with a syringe. "I'm going to give you a shot, Mr. Sage."

As the nurse smoothly injected Sage, she looked up, surprised. Sage saw the men all step back at once. Gaynel had risen from the wheelchair and was standing over Sage. She dropped to her knees beside him and leaned forward.

"I have to go away," she said, "or I can't come back. We have to lose ourselves before we can find ourselves. You know the story, David. You learned it in Sunday school."

"But, I need you," David Sage said, tears beginning to flow from his eyes.

"No you don't," Gaynel said gently. She was not wearing glasses and for the first time he saw that her eyes were really quite beautiful. She put her hand on his forehead. "Your sins are forgiven."

The crowd watch silently for a moment before Dr. Wilson broke the silence, but in a strangely subdued voice. "Give Mrs. Potts another injection and take her on down for her treatment."

Then everyone was moving. Sage tried to speak again, to tell Gaynel good-bye, but the world went far away as the sedative took effect. A moment later he was remembering, in vivid color . . .

"Unit 503," the dispatcher said.

"Go ahead," David Sage answered tiredly. It was early evening, Christmas Day, and he had been at it for fourteen hours, covering for the detectives with families. He was on his way to Shagbark to see if Larry had gotten back from his trip to Florida. He knew Ware would not be answering the phone because he was still on vacation. Veteran cops know not to answer the phone when they're trying to relax.

"Unit 503. Standby to copy a number."

Sage fished out a pen and poised it over a yellow legal pad on the seat beside him. "Go ahead," he told the dispatcher, then jotted down the number. "Can you advise what this call is in reference to?"

"Negative, Unit 503. The complainant says you were at his house early this morning and left a number."

Sage flipped open his cellular phone and punched in the numbers. The phone rang twice before it was answered. *"Hello?"*

"This is Detective Sage."

"This is Rafe Herrel. Can you come here now? Lyda did have a baby hid in her room. She's gone out to the barn with it. We heard it cryin' as she run away."

Sage hit the siren switch, called for a backup unit, and set the flashing blue strobe light up in the dash. Five minutes later he sped up the gravel driveway, throwing gravel and dust everywhere. He skidded to a stop and jumped from the car. Rafe Herrel and his wife were standing at the back of the house.

"There," the elderly man said pointing toward the tottering gray barn a hundred yards or so away. "Be careful, she may have turned some of them dogs loose!"

The barn was old with a sagging loft. Even with evening light it was dark inside. Sage drew his pistol and entered. Rottweilers were snarling on each side of him, hitting the screened dog pens that had once been horse stalls. Light was flashing from their eyes and teeth. They couldn't get to him, but he stayed in the center of the barn out of caution.

As he approached the door at the other end of the barn, he

could see light and hear more dogs snarling and growling. Slowly he pushed the splintery wooden door open and saw Lyda Herrel standing there, hands on hips, watching two huge black-and-tan rottweilers struggling over something—tearing and pulling at whatever was caught in their slobbering jaws.

As his eyes adjusted, it appeared at first that the dogs were tugging at a doll. Then the full horror assaulted him as one of the brutes pulled away a tiny arm and began to chomp on it. The other backed away, snarling, red foam dripping from its mouth, a tiny head, legs, torso and one arm gripped in its large, yellow teeth—*the mutilated remains of a baby girl, pale and bloody.*

"No! No! No!" Sage's screams filled the entire universe. He didn't hear the sound of the 9 mm rounds as he pumped them into the snarling dogs, firing until his weapon was empty.

"Don't kill my dogs!" Lyda Herrel screamed.

"You sick, evil bitch. *I'll kill you, too!"* And he might have done it, except for the fact that he couldn't seem to get another magazine into his Glock pistol. His fingers weren't working. *"Don't you know you'd be better off dropped in the ocean with a millstone around your neck, than to hurt a little child?"* Sage screamed hoarsely. The words came to him from a long-ago Sunday school lesson.

Suddenly there was a look of fear in Lyda Herrel's eyes as she watched the officer, tears running down his face, trying to reload his pistol. She turned and lumbered around the barn and out of sight.

When the patrol officer arrived, he found Sage sitting against the wall, listening to the snarling dogs in the cages along the walls. The detective was crying quietly, staring at the two dead rottweilers and the remains of the mangled infant.

David Sage woke up crying and found that his straps had been removed. But crying was all right. The dream would never return. He was healed, emptied of the pain and the guilt. He hadn't killed Lyda Herrel's baby. *She had.* It was her sin, not his.

Twenty-Two

"Well, I have no choice but to let you go," Dr. Wohlford said. "But I don't advise it." He sucked on his pipe, bouncing a neon green bow tie up and down.

"I'm healed," David Sage said. "I don't need to be here anymore. I'm going back to work."

"Dr. Wilson said you were pretty wild yesterday morning."

"Probably a reaction to the medicine I've been taking."

"What about the savior?" the psychiatrist inquired.

"Gone," Sage declared. "Something temporary, something my subconscious thought I needed. I'm fine now, and I'm ready to get out of here."

Across the room, Gaynel Potts sat smiling happily and holding her husband's hand. A girl of fourteen or so, who closely resembled Gaynel, and a little boy with glasses were chatting and smiling with her. Gaynel's hair was neatly combed, and she was wearing a cheerful yellow dress that Sage had not seen. And she was apparently wearing contact lenses rather than the thick glasses.

Dr. Chavez Wilson had taken away the dancing savior. He had run electricity through her brain, and she had come back as plain Gaynel Potts, a housewife with a nice smile. She no longer danced.

"Well, it's your choice," Wohlford said. "I'll have them prepare your discharge papers." He got up and moved over to the table where Edward was sitting.

"How are you today, Edward?"

"I'm ready to leave," Edward replied.

"That's good because I'm discharging you today."

"Might as well go. All the *interesting* people are leaving," Edward observed. "Mr. Beal and the Melted Man have gone to the veteran's hospital. Mr. Yow's transferred to a private treatment center, and Dr. Shocker has sent Katrina upstairs to be force-fed."

"There'll always be more interesting people coming in, Edward." As Dr. Wohlford finished the sentence, two orderlies brought Dr. Hart struggling down the hall.

"Let go of me, you churlish bastards. I'll have you charged with aggravated kidnapping and send you to the penitentiary!" She had been outside only two days.

"I guess you're right," Edward said. "There'll always be more interesting people—or some of the old ones coming back."

"What will you do, Edward?" Wohlford asked.

"Well, I've got a lead on a job." He glanced at Sage. "And I'm going to stay with Raymond until I get a place to live."

"Raymond Clark? You mean the recently discharged patient?"

"Yeah, I called him up and he invited me to stay."

"I see. Well, good luck, Edward, you've been an entertaining patient. Your papers will be waiting at the desk." The psychiatrist got up and moved over to the table where Rachel Cunningham was reading an old *Reader's Digest*. She turned her violet eyes toward the doctor and smiled.

"Well, I'm going to go pack, Edward. I'll give you a call after I talk to my friend in Narcotics. Remember, we met somewhere else," David Sage said.

"Gotcha," Edward said.

As Sage walked toward the door, Gaynel called out to him, "Mr. Sage, come and meet my family." Her voice was neither melodious nor squeaky. It was quite ordinary.

"This is Karen and Mike, my children, and I don't believe you've been formally introduced to my husband, George."

Sage put out his hand, hiding his aversion, and shook hands with George Potts, who was beaming. "Gaynel may be going home in a day or two," the big man said. "She says you're a cop, that right?"

"Yes I am," Sage answered. "A homicide detective."

"Guess that shows that even tough people need a little help sometimes."

"You're right," Sage agreed. "And you never know where that help will come from."

"That's right," George Potts said. "Look what the right doctor"—he threw a hateful glance at Wohlford as the doctor left the room—"did for my Gay."

"Let me wish you all the best of luck," Sage said.

He started for the door, and Rachel stepped in front of him, a mischievous smile on her face. "You weren't going to leave without giving me a kiss were you?"

"Of course not." He leaned to kiss her on the cheek, but she stepped in and gave him a quick kiss on the lips.

"I'm a big girl, and you are my hero," she said. "Remember, you're bringing your girlfriend by for dinner."

"I'll remember, Rachel."

At the counter, Nurse Grady looked up. She was wearing a smock with clowns on it. "You ready to go, David? All packed?"

"I'm all packed. I just need somebody to open the door after I get my bag."

"I'll send the orderly down." She looked at him for a moment, and her lips slid back over her extruding teeth in a smile. "I don't think you'll be back again," she said. "You look like a man finally at peace with himself."

"I *am* at peace with myself," Sage said then walked down the long gleaming hallway to his room.

There was a newspaper unfolded on the bed with a front-page story about Lyda Herrel. He tossed it into the wastebasket. Larry said it was a sting operation by God to correct the mistakes made by the criminal justice system. No matter. It was all in the past.

He picked up his bag and walked to the door where the orderly with the blond ponytail tied back with a rubber band was waiting. The man was peering out the little window. "Looks like you have a choice today."

When the door opened, Sage saw Lori and Jamey sitting on the visitor's bench, chatting. They both looked up and smiled as he walked out, then stood.

No, Sage thought, *I don't have a choice. I never did.*